Ab

The author was born ⸏
Lytham St Annes. He ⸏
Roger's journalistic
Express and Blackpool Evening Gazette before moving south
to Buckinghamshire, where he covered the great Train Robbery.

He later worked in Aylesbury and High Wycombe, later becoming the sports editor of the now defunct Evening Post at Luton, working there for ten years before joining the Sun as Midland staff man, covering soccer. He travelled extensively in Europe, covering the European Cup campaigns of Nottingham Forest and Aston Villa.

He took early retirement in 1992 to write. This is his first novel.

A former player with Tring Park C. C., he lists his interests as "cricket and playing japes." He and his wife Steve live in the pretty village of Stanton by Bridge, in Derbyshire.

You Must be Joe King!

*For my chum Rose,
who's as daft as
me and laughs a
lot ...*

[signature]

Roger Duckworth

A Square One Publication

First Published in 1995 by
Square One Publications, Saga House
Sansome Place, Worcester WR1 1UA

© Roger Duckworth 1995

British Library Cataloguing in Publication Date
Roger Duckworth
    You Must be Joe King

ISBN 1 872017 98 3

Typeset in Times by Avon Dataset Ltd, Waterloo Road,
Bidford-on-Avon B50 4JH
Printed by Antony Rowe Ltd, Chippenham, Wilts

1

Joseph King was a big chap. Big in every way. He was pushing six foot and his stomach was pushing the belt of his trousers – as if making an effort to escape. With his 30th birthday roaring towards him his rugger days were over. He could still manage the odd friendly cricket match. His short cropped hair was tousled without being untidy. He was Mr Average. He had left grammar school with a smattering of O Levels due, not to unintelligence, but to being too fond of fun and japes.

And Joseph King had never forgiven his father for calling him Joseph – when he was not even of the Roman faith, or any secular leaning for that matter. He'd run out of the times he'd sworn to belt the next bloke who said: 'You must be Joe King!'

He'd had it since junior school. Everyone thought it was original and roared in self appreciative laughter as they said it. That must have been the worst thing in his life.

The second worst thing was being bottom-of-the-pile rep with Cunliffe's Brewery – You look like a bitter man to me – try Cunliffe's . . . The advertisement hoardings were right. He was a bitter man.

No, Joe King was not a happy man right now. His heart sank when he approached his first call of the day. The rain slanted into his face as he picked his way through a minefield of metal kegs and used gas cylinders in the back yard of the Roebuck. At least the alsation was chained up this time, though it still snarled at him and showed its fearsome fangs.

This was always his worst call. The dregs of a grim area. He knew the cellar would be awash. It always was after 24 hours rain. He also knew the cooler would have packed in again and he'd have to descend into the dank, cobwebbed cavern to have yet another look at it. He also knew it would be no good as a new one had been needed for months. He winced at the thought of going home again with a white tidemark on his best black brogues. A mark that took two days polishing to remove.

Most licensees settle for a pile of bar towels and a couple of ashtrays. Not Cyril Wilson at the Roebuck. King appreciated the problem with the cooler but it was easier to pull a tiger's tooth than get anything expensive out of Cunliffe's. You'd think Wilson was running the Majestic on the sea front, where they had dinner dances and the Rotary Club met every Tuesday, rather than a back street alehouse frequented by ex-sailors, road men and your average assortment of life's unfortunates – and where the haute of cuisine aspired no further than crisps – plain or cheese and onion flavoured – and pork scratchings.

The lump of the regulars were DHSS members who never had any intention of working. They new every trick in the book when it came to signing on and explaining how many jobs they'd tried for in these hard times.

The Roebuck was a roll-your-own pub. There were more tins of Old Holborn on the tables than beer mats. The addicted seemed to have the knack of sticking the cigarette paper to their bottom lips and spreading the tobacco so thinly it went out as soon as it was put down. Hence the burn marks on the old tables. The video game and fruit machine stood gloating side by side, flashing their coloured lights to attract the gullible. And if you turned to cut out the lights they pipped and jangled. And the jukebox turned itself on every now and them to remind folk they hadn't played it for a while.

He was waiting for it. And it wasn't a long wait. 'Ah, you must be Joe King,' said portly Cyril who looked unwashed in jeans and a zip-up cardigan over an off-white T-shirt.

He laughed uproariously at his wit and looked round the bar for reaction. Half of them didn't even get it. There weren't many Mensa candidates in the public bar of the Roebuck.

This corner of north west England can be beautiful. This

was one of the grimy bits. On the right days the sunset is breathtaking. But sometimes there is a scar on a perfectly formed fruit. This was it. The Roebuck was the carbuncle on the backside of what is mostly a lovely town.

'Cooler's knackered,' said Cyril when he had recovered from his mirth. He was not conversant in the language of technical engineering. 'And I want some beer mats and ashtrays. And t'cellar door's open. Don't get your feet wet.'

'Bollocks,' said King under his breath. His collar was uncomfortably wet from the dash from car to pub. 'Can you please put the cellar light on Cyril?' he asked.

'Bulb's gone,' came the reply as King tried to negotiate the bend on the steep steps. As he eased his way off the bottom step he splashed into a flood, the cold water seeping through his lace holes. 'Bollocks,' he said again. 'This time aloud.'

The 12 year old cooler was certainly not working, Cyril had said. It was at the end of the road. And being on his patch, a new or reconditioned machine would come out of King's already sick-looking budget. That would send his targets even further into the mire, and make another mess of his commission.

He slopped back up the stairs and the daylight made him blink. That was when he discovered the white, chalky blaze down the left arm of his best business suit.

'You're right Cyril,' said King, 'It's knackered.'

'And what are you going to do about it?' the landlord asked nastily.

'We'll have to indent for another and hopefully get the fitters out tomorrow to fix it.'

'In-bloody-dent! And while you're doing your in-bloody-denting, what do I serve here?'

'Serve it warm like you've been doing for years,' chortled a jovial voice pulling his darts out of the board. 'We'll just have to sup whisky at ale prices tonight.'

'Piss off,' said the elegant Cyril. 'Just watch it chum. You've been barred once. One more yellow card and your're off.'

King left. Another happy day was gathering pace and rushing towards him. He climbed into his regulation, bottom of the market rep's Sierra 1600 and hung his jacket on the peg behind the driver's seat – as he'd been taught at his first management course. He got his white shirt even wetter in the process, but you hadn't to make a call with a crease in your suit jacket which made it look as if you'd been in a car.

One more call and sod it, King decided. He was unhappy and decided to return to the brewery to write up some long overdue reports after a flying visit to see the lovely Dora at the Wheatsheaf. It was a desirable thought. And it would get that miserable Wilson out of his teeth.

Happy, chirpy Dora admitted to being 40. Believe what you will. But she was friendly, blonde and put her brisk trade down to keeping a good pint, thanks to Pete Burns who looked after her cellars – and several other things, people said. Add to that the quality of her home made meat and potato pies and a generous cleavage which had a deal to do with her popularity. In fact she was a good all rounder.

She was warm hearted and looked cuddly. She could match any of the locals for pit-a-pat repartee. And her pub was three blocks closer to the sea front than the Roebuck. While not being exactly high class it was warm and welcoming. what a difference a landlord can make.

The Wheatsheaf also had a roaring log fire – carefully tended by the ever-willing-Peter – and sported framed photographs of old yachts and paddle steamers. There were no pictures of greyhounds or Sun calendars here.

It had no pool table so drinkers didn't keep getting jogged by the butt end of cues. The fruit machine and video race track were in a side room frequented by the kids, many of them under-aged. There was nothing strident to stop the bar front banter.

Talk in the lounge was more weather, football and cricket. It was still a corner pub, but a homely one.

King still didn't feel like facing the sales director. It was not only Cyril's cooler, but the reports which he had been asked for several times, worrying him. He donned his chalk-stained jacket and splashed into the front bar.

4

'Aye up chuck,' beamed Dora. 'Been fishing?'

'Only in the dark – in the Roebuck cellar,' replied King, warming his backside in front of the hot and welcome fire.

'Anything you want Dora?' asked King, realising immediately he'd said the wrong thing. He cursed his naivety. He knew what was coming next from the Brook Street blonde.

She didn't fail him. 'Well, what're you doing this afternoon?' she grinned cheekily. 'We shut at three.'

King, used to her, said, 'Haven't time today love, but if you want any bar towels, ashtrays or pump sparklers I've got a bootful. That's all I've got time for today. I've got to see his lordship this afternoon, and that probably means another bollocking.'

Foggy Fenwick, droll, bar-room wit, who seemed to be in his corner between the collection box for the blind and the mild pump morning and night, chipped in, 'I don't know how you stick that old bastard Evans, Joe. Is everyone scared of Julian bloody Evans? I'd tell him to stuff it.'

'You forget there's a recession Foggy. A lot of people are having a rough time. I've a mortgage, a wife and two ankle biters. The bills need paying and they all need feeding and clothing. I know what you're saying though. I've been thinking about it a bit. And I've had about enough of his nibs. Hey Dora, give us a half of Nigerian lager.'

'Nigerian what?' she said, falling straight for it.

'Guinness, you dopey tart.' King was beginning to feel more human. At least his collar had dried. And his backside was warm.

'Fancy a game of arrows?' asked Foggy. 'Loser gets Dora for the afternoon.'

'You cheeky sod,' laughed the happy licensee. 'Let Joe go and play conductors.'

King looked at her blankly. 'Conductors?'

'Face the bleedin' music,' she grinned.

'I thought you were telling him to get on the bus and head for the hills,' said Foggy.

'That might be closer to the truth that you think,' murmured

King. 'In the meantime I've got to get back to GCHQ and account for the beer that's not been drunk this month. That old sod seems to think you can drag them in off the street, pour Cunliffe's bitter down their necks and pluck the money out of their pockets.'

Back at Brook Street he was chatting to his pal Jock Henderson, a fellow rep.

'I've had to hit more targets than Robin Hood. If I ever move on I won't go into the managed house side of it again. You have to feel sorry for the licensees. You give them a target and if they work themselves into the ground and hit it, you set them another – or put their rents up. God, what a game.'

2

The clouds seemed darker and lower over the brewery than anywhere else in town to King. If some of the pubs in his area were back street, headquarters was one worse. It was at the back of town behind the rail yard, cut off by the canal as if to make it a long way round. Some customers suspected the water for the brew came straight out of the cut. They were probably right. It was one way to save on water rates and slow the meter down.

If ever a chap needed cheering up it was Joe King that wet March morning. As he dragged himself up the general office he had a heavy heart. And it was even heavier when Jenny Bottomley, the long legged, long serving secretary announced: 'He wants to see you.' Jenny was a pal to all the lads out in the field. She warned them when to keep their heads down – and what to expect. It was sort of preparation, like being told to put an exercise book down the back of your pants when the headmaster summons you.

'What's he want Jen?' asked King. 'Is it serious?'

'Targets, figures I think. He asked me for the files.'

'Shit,' said King with feeling. It was like being told by Moneypenny that M was waiting for James Bond, wanting to know where he'd been, why he'd been so long – and to cut down on his alcohol intake. He wished she had a hat stand and he had a hat he could casually flip on it from four yards as he breezed in.

'Ah, Mr King,' said Evans, who could manage to look malevolent without practice. This time he looked more than usually pernicious. His thin lips went with his thin face. Above the unsmiling gap with a bit of a moustache that looked as if it had taken a lot of producing.

It seemed that his main pleasure in life, after a weekend round of golf at which he could not even get a handicap, was reminding people he was sales director – and the brewery's raison d'etre was to sell beer. As a general and leader, he commanded five reps who had to service 46 managed houses between them. His other big pleasure was being offhand.

He would no more think of going out for a lunchtime drink with one of his team than joining a circus as a high wire act. Julian Evans was not a good advert for his product – something that was supposed to make people happy and relaxed. He was universally disliked, from the sales force, through the office staff, his acquaintances at the gold club and, many believed, his mousy wife Mavis.

And he especially didn't like Joe King – perhaps because he was popular. He still suspected it was King who pulled the egg trick on him, a jape that left him the laughing stock of the Brook Street brewery.

King used to think about it in his lowest moments. He could even make himself laugh out loud. It was, in fact, a corker.

Every day Evans lunched at his desk. He always had the same – a yoghurt, a banana, a slice of wholemeal bread and a hard boiled egg. He always ate them in the same order.

King may not have been the best seller in Brook Street, but he had a rare eye for a laugh. It was possibly a hangover from his days in the fifth form.

Every Friday Evans presented himself at the heads of department meeting in the boardroom. This particular morning in a rare oversight, he left his office door open. And there on his leather-topped mock Regency desk was his little yellow Tupperware lunch box, a bottle of Perrier water standing sentry at its side.

King weighed up the possibilities and decided it was too good to miss. 'Hey, look there,' he grinned at his colleague in misery Jock. 'Just sit tight and cover for me Jock.'

King nipped up the back stairs to the works canteen and

called Monica, the kindly soul behind the servery who always gave him extra custard – on the rare occasions he was in the building for lunch.

'Hey, Monica, give us an egg,' whispered King.

Monica looked perplexed to say the least. 'Fried, boiled, scrambled or poached?' she asked. 'Are you going to make soldiers?'

'None of those,' said King. 'Just a fresh egg.'

Monica looked at him strangely. 'You've been under a bit of stress haven't you?' But she picked a large egg out of the tray near the hot sizzler and passed it over. King put it carefully into the jacket pocket of his rep's suit and went back down to the general office.

'What you up to Joe?' asked Jock. 'Have you finally flipped? Gone over the top?'

'Just watch the far door,' said King. 'If bollock chops appears give me a whistle and I'll pretend I was looking for him.'

King strolled nonchalantly into Evans' office and took the lid off the little plastic box, removed the hard-boiled egg and replaced it with a fresh one. He pocketed the hard boiled egg and returned to his desk. 'Now we just sit back and wait for the fun.'

'Oh my God,' said Jock. 'This could be curtains.'

'Just wait. Here comes the fun,' said King.

Evans strode briskly back to his office looking prim, not even nodding good-day to the two reps sitting there.

It had obviously been a good meeting. good for him any way. He would have heaped the blame of any fall in managed house sales on his men. He always did. God knows what the MD must think he was employing. Surely the top man couldn't believe ALL the bullshit.

Evans returned to his desk, his door still open, and arranged his little daily picnic on the desk in front of him.

The banana was fastidiously unzipped and digested. Then out came the slice of brown bread and the egg.

'Oh my Christ,' muttered Jock, peeping through his fingers.

With a sharp crack on the leading edge of his desk, Evans split the shell. But instead of the usual splintering the lot smashed. Yolk and white shot down his shirt front, jacket and carefully pressed trousers.

'Jesus Christ,' said Jock.

Evans screeched: 'Bloody hell. The stupid bloody woman.' He turned puce and, after wiping himself down the best he could with his white linen hankie, he snatched up the telephone.

'You stupid bloody cow,' he bellowed into the phone. 'You didn't boil my egg and it's all over my sodding suit . . . Don't you argue with me woman. If you're that sure you boiled it you must have put it back in the tray and given me the wrong one. Bovine bugger.'

Evans slammed down the phone. King and Jock were besides themselves with mirth at their desks in the general office. Joe could contain himself no longer and let out a powerful roar of pent-up laughter. Jack joined in and they had to leave the office. They didn't escape before Evans spotted them rocking with laughter and stared after them balefully and suspiciously.

Outside in the yard the pair had to hang on to each other. Both were by now aching with the effort of trying to stop their uncontrollable glee. 'She'll be going through the tray now, shaking every bloody egg,' gasped King. 'Jesus, she's going to get some when he gets home.'

'You don't think he suspects us?' said Jock. 'I've got a huge mortgage.'

'Never,' said King, somewhat uncertainly. 'How could he? He can't bring the finger-print squad in for that mess. He didn't know whether to shit himself or wind his watch. But for Christ's sake keep mum. Don't even let it out in the bottling plant. You know what that lot are like.'

After a pie and a pint at the Anchor, the twosome returned to base and King tapped on Evans' now closed door.

'Enter,' he heard him bark.

'You wanted to see me?' asked King.

'Yes I did,' said the sales director, his piggy little eyes boring into the face of the suddenly uncomfortable-feeling King.

A week had passed since the egg incident and there had been a sort of strained air about the place. 'What's the matter?'

'The matter? The bloody matter! I'll tell you what the matter is. It's your figures. God knows what you're telling these managers, but it's certainly not on the improvement in keeping our product or selling it in any great amounts. Look.'

Evans bent down and opened the bottom drawer of his mock Regency desk, extricated a manila file on the front of which it said: 'Area J. King.' He slammed the drawer, obviously delighted to have hooked King on the end of his line.

In the process of his irritable actions his striped gold club tie caught in the drawer. Suddenly it was Evans who was on the end of the line. Well hooked.

When Evans tried to straighten he almost strangled himself. The thickness of the tie meant he couldn't pull it out of the tightly fitting drawer. It almost meant he couldn't open the drawer. He turned red as he tugged, his struggling served only to tighten the knot at his neck.

King weighed up the situation – and started to laugh. His stomach wobbled in merriment as Evans got redder. 'If you get out of that we'll call you Houdini,' gasped King, holding his belly. By this time he knew he was in for it anyway.

'Jenny,' choked Evans. 'Get in here.' By now his voice was but a croak and the secretary didn't hear his mayday calls. He looked at King in total embarrassment, but was too proud to ask him for help.

King beamed: 'Shall I get Jenny?' Evans nodded, and the helpless King staggered away from the scene to find the secretary. He didn't run. For once he was on top of the situation with the boss.

When he reached Jenny's desk he said weakly: 'Miserable morning Jen, but it's looking up.' He had to wipe the tears from his eyes.

'What the hell's the matter with you Joe?' asked the pretty blonde looking up from her keyboard and screen.'

'The boss wants to see you. And I'd take a pair of scissors,' chortled King. 'But there's no hurry.'

But Jenny, valuing her job guessed that the opposite was the case. She took the scissors from the top drawer of her desk and headed for Evans's office. 'These the scissors he uses to cut expenses, Jen?' asked King cheekily. When she reached the scene of the calamity she couldn't believe her eyes.

King, who had followed at a safe distance watched the scene with interest and undisguised joy. By this time Evans could no longer speak. He just managed to point to his neck from his crouched position. He looked like a modern Quasimodo.

Jenny was far from daft. It must have been surprise that prompted the question: 'What on earth's the matter Mr Evans. What are you doing?' King stood in the doorway and said as seriously as he could: 'I think he's stuck. Perhaps you should snip his tie off before he hangs himself.'

Jenny walked round the desk, quickly evaluated the situation and cut Evans' red and blue golf club tie asunder close to his neck. 'There we are,' she said, leaving the room tactfully.

Evans was unable to pull himself together for a full minute. And a minute can be an eternity in a tense situation.

Then he spat: 'That wasn't very bloody dignified for a sales director, was it King? Why do things always happen when you're around? I still think you had something to do with that egg business.'

'Egg business?' King asked with all the innocence of a Hollywood actor being given the third degree down at the precinct. 'I don't know to what you are alluding.'

'Don't get clever dickie with me, King. You're not that bloody smart. That's why you're in here right now. It's these figures. Our sales increase on your patch are lower than your exes. Just how many beers do you buy people? We are not a charitable organisation. We're here to sell the flaming stuff, not treat all our chums to it in various seedy back street pubs.'

'It's promotional,' said King. 'I can't help the area I've been given. I like to think if I buy someone a half of best he'll get the taste and swill back pints of the stuff when I've left.'

'By the time you leave, King, they'll be past buying anything – except a taxi fare home. You'd better start getting a few results or . . .'

The sales manager left the threat unuttered. But Joe King got the drift. On leaving Evans' office he headed for the car park, bumping into Henderson on the way.

'I've had enough of that bastard, Jock, I'm up to here,' said King holding his right hand at a level near his nose.

'Let's go out for a half. At least I've got something to make you laugh.'

The pair drove in King's company Sierra to the Majestic to enjoy a bit of comfort. As the pair walked through the swing door Henderson was still hooting with laughter at the tale of Evans' tie.

'I don't know how you get away with it Joe,' his friend said. 'But don't go over the top with him. Don't push your luck too far. You need this job. We all do. Just because we are working for an arsehole, and you can't predicate for a complete arsehole, we still need the cash – even if it is only peanuts.'

'If I wanted paying in peanuts I'd join the zoo,' retorted King.

'Okay mate, but think. What would you do? You're what, 30? You've got a young family and there's no work about – not your sort anyway. You're not exactly a tradesman or the sort of wee man who could do a heavy humping job.

'At least this is soft. It takes you into pubs and you're given a smart motor to belt around in. At least we're out and about, not superglued to an office desk. What the hell could you do anyway? You ain't exactly got a degree in nuclear physics. Nor are you in demand as a brain surgeon.'

'Point taken Jock,' said King. 'But I've got the worst patch in the company. My bonuses are about non-existent because people are drinking less, not more at the moment. And I've got that bastard on my back all the time. If I produced miracles he'd still hate me. And I do have a bit of an idea. I've always liked writing. I tried to be a journalist in my teens, but there were no jobs going. The only reason I'm doing this is for survival. But things are changing a bit. The kids are a little older. And after school they're happy to go to their gran's for an hour or so – and she likes to see them. Because of this Maggie has pulled a nice little job as a dental receptionist. She starts next week.'

'She ought to be able to pull there,' joked Jock. 'So what is this great idea you've got to make your fortune?'

'A pub crawl,' grinned King. 'Pick a route, get the maps out and go on a crawl – say for a month.'

Henderson looked at him as if he'd been taking something strange imported from the far east and had escaped detection at customs.

'Aye man. That sounds great. Should make you a fortune this pub crawling – if you don't spend one first. At least you'll end up good at darts. You might even get on Bull's Eye on telly. Have you lost your marbles?'

'You know Foggy Fenwick who goes in the Wheatsheaf? Well, he's been having headaches – and it's nothing to do with our bitter.

'He's got to go in for a brain scan soon. I'll get him to make you an appointment. Have you gone crackers man? Has Evans sent you over the edge? Are you really serious about chucking it all in to go on a flaming pub crawl? God man, you go on one every day. What are you going to use for money?'

King took a sip of his bitter and knocked back his Scotch chaser. He held up his hand. 'Hold on me old mate. That's where the writing bit comes in. I fancy going on the biggest pub crawl ever. I'd like to think I could write about what I've seen. The characters, the crack at the bar, the beer, the landlords. All I need is the guts to do it.

'I need to know Maggie can manage for a month. I'd like to think I can find something else when I've finished the project. I've already sent off a few hush-hush letters to other breweries. All I need to know is a friendly publisher. They may be a bit thin on the ground.'

'Ooh, there's a rub,' said Jock. 'You've no experience. No name as a journalist. You don't even know you can do it. You'll end in debtors' prison or the workhouse. Think about it buddy. Can you get yourself a sponsor? How are you going to travel? Who pays for the car – or B and Bs. What are you going to do, take a bloody wigwam and some dry wood? I can't see you existing on a billycan of baked beans over a camp fire. Our current existence may be shitty – but it's a living.

'Just let Evans' jibes and bollockings bounce off you. Try the old army trick of when the sergeant major has his nose against yours and is shouting abuse, just say to yourself: "And you, shithouse".'

King re-ordered and returned to the table in the bay window, and looked at the waves lashing over the sea wall. And a bit of doubt began to seep in.

'I'll promise you one thing cock, I'll do nothing hasty. It's going to need a lot of thinking about. And I've got to get it over to Maggie. Right chum, shall we go back to base or go to the Roebuck and fight a few sailors?'

'Jeez man,' said Jock. 'Let's get the hell back while we've both got a job. Think of that pay cheque at the end of the month. And if you want a sponsor for your balmy idea, try the Beano.'

King grinned, punching his pal playfully on the shoulder. 'All will be revealed,' he said.

3

Joe and Maggie King lived on the edge of town in a respectable superb, in a respectable semi in an avenue where all the houses looked the same – apart from the curtains. After a few beers you could find yourself trying to unlock the door next door but one.

They all had well shaved front lawns and garden sheds at the back. King had heard Orchard Road described as 'All privet hedges and dog shit.'

Maggie was a neat person, a good mother to Jason and Heather, a good cook and enthusiastic gardener, a trait fuelled by her penchant for tidiness.

She was black haired, pretty in a sensible sort of way and spoke with a barely discernible Lancashire accent.

The kids were your average kids. Not over-bright, not dull. Jason was an avid football fan, glued to the television on Sunday afternoons and at eight years old couldn't wait to get into Class 4 to have a chance to get in the junior school team.

Heather, six, was well, six. Vivacious and just joining the mainstream of school life.

When he got home that night King saw the kids off to bed and sat down for dinner with Maggie – trays in front of the telly. 'Well, Joe,' she said. 'I start at the surgery on Monday. That'll make things a bit easier.'

'I've had another run in with that bastard Evans. There are times when I think of chucking it all in,' said King. He was really just putting a toe in the water to test the temperature.

'Good God Joe, don't talk like that,' said Maggie, 'what the hell would you do?'

'Oh, I'd find something else,' he replied defensively. 'Let's have a bottle of wine.'

He could see straight away this wasn't going to be easy. He could see himself being mown down as he made his run for the wire. 'Just heard the weather forecast,' he said, now wanting to change the subject. 'They say it'll either rain or go dark before morning.'

'They only put the hour forward at the weekend. We'll have to be getting out in that garden in the next week or so,' said Maggie. King groaned inwardly. There was no chance he could say anything more about his scheme.

Jock was right, he needed cash in the bank and a friendly publisher. And could he do it well enough? Did they bother with re-writes at these places? He doubted it. You had to be right first time. He felt trapped between the rock and the hard stuff. Joe King didn't sleep well that night. Job on the line, not much future, home and family to maintain. How the hell could he get out before he was pushed. That was a real scrap heap situation at his age. Did he make a run for it or get shot in the back?

The next morning he felt terrible. Too much beer yesterday and wine last night. A rotten night. Responsibility was getting to him. They got the kids off to school, Joe polished the last of the tidemarks off his black brogues, kissed Maggie goodbye and headed for Brook Street.

Jenny had already put the list of calls for the day on his desk. At least it didn't include the Roebuck. Their new cooler must still be working. Joe breezed in after him: 'What-ho Joe. Packed your tent. Got a road map?'

'Piss off.' That was how King felt that morning. He had a sense of foreboding and decided to get off the premises before pinched-faced Evans arrived. He just made it, driving out of the car park as the sales manager drove in. That was too bloody close, he thought. Now who first?

It looked like drizzle again and he decided to try to start the day with a chuckle and pulled up outside the Wheatsheaf. Dora was getting the milk in. 'Coffee Chuck?' she offered.

'Please,' said King. 'Any problems?'

'I just need a good man love,' she grinned. 'Any offers?'

'Christ Dora, I've about enough on my plate as it is at the moment. But I'll remember your kind offer.'

By lunchtime he had almost worked through his list. Nothing exciting, the usual complaints about cloudy bitter, a message from the Dog and Duck in Love Street that a barrel of mild was off and needed changing. Would he see to it straight away?

He gave away the usual hoard of mats and ashtrays and details of a new competition whereby a lucky couple could have a free fortnight in the Bahamas if they bought the right ticket and scraped the right squares off their silver foil. They all fell for it every time at 10p a go. And every year they forgot that there hadn't been a winner last year.

This prize was more elusive than newspaper bingo or Spot the Ball. All they'd ever done was list the runners up who each won six pints of Cunliffe's bitter. That crafty bastard Evans. No doubt he'd dreamed it up, and King wondered if the sales manager had ever been to the Bahamas . . .

It was while he was at the Dog and Duck that the phone rang and the lass behind the bar said: 'It's your office Joe. Can you go back.'

King's heart hit the bottom of his stomach. What had he done now? What a way to spend a life. He seemed to be lurching from one disaster to another. Thank God he had a happy home. 'If there were no ladies present I'd say it,' said Joe.

The barmaid grinned and said: 'Let it go Joe. Have this one on me.' Joe did. And he said it very loudly, causing the domino players in the other bar to pause in their game. And that took some doing.

King dragged his heavy heart to his car and drove through the drizzle and the dull streets. He crossed the canal bridge and into the yard where there seemed a lot of manpower activity.

When he reached the general office all the staff were gathered, the reps, the wages department, and the usual odds and ends of staff that oil the wheels of industry so thoroughly.

'What's going on Joe?' King asked his pal.

'Well, there's talk of redundancy. It seems the brewery's in the shit.'

'You mean the likes of you and me are in it,' said King 'Some'll be alright.'

'I think it's worse than that Joe, from what I hear. I was talking to old Pete Walker, and after 26 years here as head brewer there's nothing he doesn't know. Things are apparently bad at top level. The MD and a couple of the trades union people are coming to talk to us.'

'Bloody hell, you mean . . .?'

'Could be,' said Jock. 'We'll just have to wait and see. You might really have something to moan about by the end of the day.'

The mood in the office was tense. Nobody had much to say, they were wrapped in their own thoughts. Family men, youngsters saving to get married, elderly work-horses who had spent most of their days at Cunliffe's.

'Well, we'll soon know,' said Jock, nodding towards the double doors at the end of the room. Striding grim-faced along the corridor was MD Richard McGee. In the platoon following him were Evans, then the production director, then the financial director, then the two union representatives. One for the white collar workers, the other for the workforce down in the brewhouse.

You could have pierced the air with a penknife. 'What I have to say is not pleasant, not pleasant for any single one of us,' said McGee, positioning himself at the front of the assembly.

'I am here to make a statement. I shall not be answering any questions today. It is simply this. The Official Receiver has been called into Cunliffe's Brewery which finds itself in a state of bankruptcy after 65 years of trading, during which time we feel we have served the community with good beer, goodwill and good grace.

'At this time I cannot say whether there will be any takeover bid. There has been no sign of one so far, and our position in the market has been known among the higher echelons of the trade for some time.

'From lunchtime today we are effectively out of business and your notices will be served forthwith. Should you be of a mind, you are all at liberty to re-apply for your posts if the brewery goes into production again. But that is unlikely.

'Your P45 forms, National Health records and pay until the end of the month will be posted to you. I am deeply sorry for you all and wish to thank you for your hard work for Cunliffe's over the years.

'There will, of course be redundancy payments for every member of the staff, based on length of service. This is being worked out at this moment. Details of payment and a full breakdown, along with your cheques will be available at the window in the wages department at noon tomorrow. Thank you all again, and good luck.'

McGee and his battalion turned about and marched out, presumably to deliver the same message down in the brewhouse. There was a stunned silence in the office. It was broken by a heartfelt sob from Jenny.

King walked across to her and put a kind arm round her shoulders. 'Come on kid, that'll do no good. A lass like yourself with your ability and sexy looks will walk into another job.'

'Thanks Joe,' she said and kissed him on the cheek. 'What will you do? You've got a young family.'

'Something will turn up,' he said and walked across to Jock: 'It's your round pal,' he said. 'Let's go and drown them. I'll just give Maggie a ring first.'

The phone in Orchard Road was picked up after the first ring. 'Maggie, I've got a bit of bad news,' he said.

'Oh Joe, I know. It's just been on the local news. What are you doing?'

We're going for a pint and a chat and then I'll be back. I won't be long. Keep smiling.' King put down the phone in a daze. It had all been so quick.

Unable to face Dora's fun and friendship the two pals retired to the posh bar of the Majestic. 'Well, Egon Ronay, you'll be able to take the open road now,' said Jock trying to make light of the bleak situation.

'What about you Jock?'

'Let's just wait and see what the redundancy comes to,' said the Scot.

Several pints and chasers later they threaded their separate ways home, sharing a taxi. At least their company cars had not been collared yet, and King left his locked safely in the car park after a word with the manager.

He knew what he faced when he got home. It wasn't as bad as he had expected. The sensible Maggie had got on with preparing dinner and poured herself a family-size gin and tonic. But Joe could see she'd had a weep and that there was a tremble in her hand that clutched the glass.

'Well Joe, you said you wanted out. Now you've got it. Any ideas?'

'A few,' said King. 'There's going to be some redundancy. Let's see how much that comes to first. I've got a bit of an idea about writing.'

'Writing! You couldn't even write those reports for old Evans.'

'Aye, but that wasn't lack of ability, it was lack of drive and motivation – and being treated like a doormat. Don't fret lass. When the kids come home I'll tell them all about it. And we'll ask Helen to come and sit in later and go out to that Cantonese for a meal.'

'God Joe, you're out of work, and I've put the dinner on.'

'Give the kids what they want and we'll heat the rest up tomorrow.'

Maggie still wasn't sure, but agreed. Tomorrow was another day. It certainly was in their house tonight.

And Joe King knew he was at the junction on the main line of his life. What he had yearned for for so long was now almost a possibility. As he and Maggie sat in the elegant comfort of the Keng Wong, still laughing over their attempts to master chopsticks, Joe raised his glass and said, 'Here's to a fat cheque – and bollocks to Evans.'

'Joe!' grinned Maggie in mock disgust. Then she chuckled: 'I'll drink to that.'

They had breakfast with the kids and as Joe cracked his boiled egg the sun sneaked out from behind the cloud and grinned down on him. 'See that,' he said. 'It's a whole new world. And don't you kids worry. We're not skint you know. And mum starts her job on Monday.'

'Does that mean she won't be here when we come home.' asked Heather, looking alarmed.

'Don't worry about that love,' he said. 'You can go and see your Nan for an hour each evening. You know you like that. No eating all her toffees, mind. You'll be coming home for your tea.'

Little Heather's face lit up. 'That's OK,' she said, relief showing on her face.

'Now off with you. Mind the road. Don't talk to strangers. I'll be here when you come home tonight. Enjoy your school dinner.' He kissed them both and looked at Maggie.

'Well, kiddo, it's decision day,' he said. 'I'm going to collect the car and meet Jock. We're going to together to find out if we've been worth our weight in gold to Cunliffe's beers, the nectar of the north.'

4

The two pals met in the car park. 'How're you feeling pal?' said Jock.

'Okay. A bit numb. I'll be glad when we've got this over. We'll clear our desks first. I'm not standing in any bloody queues at wages. I wouldn't queue for a Cup final ticket, so sod this. Can't you see it Jock, a listless parade of glum faces – and everyone comparing cheques, arguing as to who has been there the longer and where they stood in the rank of heirachy. Balls, I think I'm just going to say a fond farewell to Evans, if he's still here,' said King pointedly.

'Watch it pal,' said Jock. 'Don't do anything you'll regret. Remember, you might find yourself working for him again. Christ, there may even be a takeover yet.'

'Sure,' said King. 'Let's go and see how the land lies. Let's see if the queue's gone.'

The pair went up to the sombre general office. King was more cheerful than Henderson. He felt as you must after release from a stretch in Strangeways.

King sat in his desk for probably the last time. He went through his drawers, pocketed his digital calculator, used over the years to work out his 'fiddle sheets'. He opened the last drawer, shouldered in the bottom left hand corner of his desk and let out a roar of laughter.

There is was. The egg. The elusive hard boiled egg. He'd forgotten all about it since his infamous switch. Henderson looked up in astonishment. 'Glad you find it's funny, wee man,' he said gravely.

King held up the egg. After a second the Scot joined him in

guffaws. 'Get rid of the bloody thing Joe,' he said. 'It's incriminating evidence.'

It was deposited under screwed up papers in a waste bin at the far end of the room. 'We mustn't be connected with that, must we?' said King.

Evans' office door was still closed. King decided to go for his fond farewell – just to show there was no malice! He opened the door and marched in. Pinch-faced Evans was at his desk and looked surprised at the intrusion, banging his top drawer shut in an expression of guilt. There was a crunch of breaking glass and Evans looked down in a mixture of shock and hatred at the amber liquid seeped through the crack between the two pieces of plywood that formed the base of the drawer.

'Shit,' he said with deep feeling. 'I don't know how you bloody do it King!'

'I've just come in to say cheerio,' grinned King cheekily. 'See you around Mr Evans. Nasty smell of broken glass round here!'

He headed back to Henderson in triumph. He'd won the battle with his old opponent in the last round.

Jock was talking to Jenny. 'Hey, guess what, Evans is a secret drinker. No wonder he never wanted to go out and visit his area or meet the rep's "on site".'

Between laughs he told the couple what had happened, 'Oh dear,' said Jenny. 'I'd put some new glasses in his hospitality drinks cabinet. I think he used to have the odd nip now and then and put the glass in his top draw to he could close it if the MD or anyone else went in. The new glasses must have been a bit taller than the old ones and the drawer wouldn't close on them. And to think I only changed them last week because the other crystal was getting a bit chipped round the edges . . .'

King's stomach was lurching about again. 'That bugger's certainly chipped,' he chuckled. 'He must bloody love me. He's made my life a misery on occasions, but I guess, one way and another, we've ended all square. The tale of the egg, the tie and the glass. Bloody hell.' The threesome stood, heads together, arms around each other and laughed together.

Evans did not reappear and King and Henderson went up to wages. It was like the last walk. 'You first Jock,' said King. 'You have seniority.'

Henderson collected his envelope and King followed. 'Any left for me, Angie?' he said to the amiable clerk, who was also out on her neck. She handed him a white envelope through the barred window.

King turned to his mate, who was about to rip his envelope open: 'Not here Jock,' he said quietly. 'Let's get this place out of our hair. Do you realise we've still got our company cars. Let's get them out of the yard before we're asked for the keys. Then we'll do it right – in the front lounge of the Majestic. And if they want their bloody cars they'll have to come and find them.'

As they walked across the yard towards the parking area, the pair were approached by a couple of young men, one with a camera and a heavy-looking bag slung over his shoulder.

The other one said: 'Excuse me, Evening Press. Are you among the unfortunates who have been made redundant by the brewery?'

'We are,' said Jock. 'Many years service between us.'

'My name is Frank Hilton. I'm a reporter. Willie here, as you will have noticed is a snapper. Will you do a piece with us?'

'Why not Joe,' said Henderson, looking at his mate. 'A bit of publicity may have them lining up waiting to employ us.' King shrugged his agreement.

'May I have a shot of you leaving for the last time?' asked Willie. 'Will you stand under the Cunliffe's sign and hold your hands out in a gesture of despair, or something.'

'No question about it, despair has crept in,' grinned King and he and his chum posed for the camera.

'What are you going to do now?' asked Frank, after all the routine questions about service and families.

'I haven't a clue,' said Jock. 'Just a matter of seeing what blows up in the wind.'

'And you,' said Hilton looking at King. 'What will you do?'

'I'm going on a pub crawl,' he said.

'A what? Well, that's one day out of the way. What about the rest of your life?'

'No lad,' said King. 'You've got it wrong. I'm going on a month's pub crawl.'

'A month, eh? I'll warn the clinic,' grinned the young reporter. 'When do you start?'

'I'm not joking,' said King, though he had to smile as he said it. 'I've always wanted a go at your job. There just weren't the opportunities at the time. I'm hoping to organise a 100-mile tour, taking in the interesting pubs and characters; talk to the nutters; test their beef and dumplings – the pub's, not the nutters. Then I'm going to write it up and hope to find someone to publish it. Give that a mention in your piece and I'll buy you a pint next time I see you. You never know, it may just spark a bit of action somewhere.'

'When are you starting this great adventure?' asked Hilton.

'As soon as I know how much money I have and can organise a vehicle. Sorry, we've got to go. Got a date on the prom – and it ain't in a shelter.'

'A date?' said Hilton.

'Aye, at the Majestic,' said Henderson. 'See you around.'

The pair sat in their favourite bay window, their beer and their white envelopes untouched and unopened in front of them. 'That's our future,' said Jock. 'Let's see how long it will last.'

They opened their envelopes together. Their P45's and official notice were there. Then there was another smaller envelope. Like those they got their monthly pay cheques in.

King found his hand trembling slightly as he pulled the gummed top open. He extricated a cheque and looked at the figure in the little box in the bottom right had corner. He blinked, and did a double take.

'Jesus Christ Jock,' he said. 'Five and a half grand. I expected about half that – especially with my record. How about you?'

'Six,' said Jock. 'Six bloody grand. I'm wealthy. Bloody hell man, have a double.'

'Get them in,' said King. 'I'm going to ring Maggie.' She answered the phone nervously. 'Are you OK Joe?'

'We're rich beyond the dreams of avarice,' said King. 'Five and a half grand. That'll keep the dogs off the doorstep for a bit.'

Maggie was silent. Then she laughed. 'I saw the sun come out this morning. Now we have a bit of breathing space to sort things out. Where are you?'

'The Majestic with Jock. We came here to open our cheques together. And oh yes! I saw Evans for the last time. He was throwing whisky all over himself. I'll tell you later. But the bastard didn't beat me.'

'Okay love, when will you be back?'

'About three. I want to pick up the Press. They were down there interviewing us all this morning. Jock and I could be famous.' King explained to his wife what had happened with the couple from the paper and said: 'See you in a bit.'

Back at the table he grinned: 'Cheers Jock. I feel like a tiger who's found the door of his cage left open. Look, we'll have a couple here and a sandwich to soak it up and see if we're in the news on the way home.'

King went into the newsagent's shop and took the top two copies off the pile of Press's. And there they were. A big picture on the front page, and the headline blared: 'Last round for brewery workers.'

The story began: 'A brewery rep who found himself in the gutter after the 65 year old Cunliffe's Brewery folded yesterday, hopes to become a writer.

'Joseph King, 30, is planning a month's pub crawl to look into life around the country's locals.

'He said this morning: "I've always had a journalist in me trying to get out. And if you're going to start again, you may as well start with something you know about. I know quite a lot about pubs".'

The story went on at length, quoting Jock and the lads in the brewhouse they had interviewed.

'Bloody, bloody hell,' said King as he and Henderson stood

outside the shop. 'What, for Christ's sake, is Maggie going to say about this? My God. I've done it now. Have you got a spare bed?'

'Not a bad picture,' laughed Jock. Bed? Mannie, you've made yours, go and lie on it. We'll have a chat tomorrow when the dust has settled – or the shit will have hit the fan. Noon at the Majestic.' He drove off, leaving King to panic alone.

As he drove home Joe was making up excuses, and rejecting them as fast as they flashed in front of him. How could he put this to Maggie? His scheme seemed wild now it was out in black and white. Maggie was in the kitchen. She turned and smiled and gave him a kiss as he went in. 'How do you feel now it's all over love?' she asked.

She had obviously not yet seen the Evening Press. Joe slipped his copy into the inside pocket of his mac which he put in the cloakroom.

'Oh, I'm Okay. Good pay off eh? I just need time to think – and a bit of fresh air. I think I'll have a walk round the block.' He donned an anorak and went out of the front door. 'I guess I'm right in it now,' he said to himself.

When he returned in 20 minutes Maggie was still in the kitchen. But when she turned her countenance was very different.

'What's going on Joe?' she asked. 'I've just had ever such a funny phone call. Someone claiming to be the news editor of the Evening Press. He said he wants to talk to you about a pub crawl or something. He said will you ring back. He's called Keith something or other. His number's by the phone. I can't help thinking you're up to something Joseph King,' she said.

Joe pretended to look daft, which wasn't difficult, and telephoned the number on the pad. He asked for the news editor. 'Keith Harris,' said a voice above the babble of a busy sounding office.

'Oh yes, Joe, good of you to ring so quickly. Have you seen the paper tonight?'

'You could say that,' said King.

'Well, perhaps we can have a chat. We might just be

interested in doing something with your stuff if it's what we want.'

'You mean print it?' said King.

'If it's right,' Harris repeated. 'There'd be a few bob in it plus exes if it's any good. If it's not it's spiked. Can you come and see me at 2pm tomorrow?'

'I'll look forward to it,' said King and they rang off.

He could now come clean with Maggie. They never hid anything from each other anyway and he was wondering how to broach the subject. The sun sure had shone on him that March morning.

5

'What are you up to mister?' said Maggie, walking through from the kitchen. What's all this crawling and newspapers – and you going off?'

King showed her the evening paper. 'You're as soft as a chocolate cream, Joe,' she said. Brewery rep to travel writer in one fell swoop!'

Joe laughed, partly with relief now it was all out. 'Listen Pet,' he said. 'You know I've always wanted to do a bit of writing. Well, I had this idea. This is my chance. The reporter of the Evening Press picked it up and put it to his editor apparently. I'm going to get paid for going on a journey across the north somewhere. I have to talk to folks in the pubs and market places. Send them back a taste of life out there. I'm going to get expenses as well. I'm going to do it for a month. But I'm not going that far and I can be back at the weekends – even in between if there's any problem. It would be daft to dump the idea. I'm going for it.'

Maggie looked at him lovingly and said: 'You do that Joe. One month mind. This may be your chance chum, but don't mess it up. Get yourself organised.'

Joe looked at Maggie and said: 'Look love, we've got five and a half grand. I'm going to put it in the bank now. I shall then make a cheque out to you for five thousand for the house-keeping. I'll take the other five hundred to cover myself. Whatever's left at the end goes back in the kitty. How's that?'

Maggie smiled. She knew how miserable Joe had been. 'Go and blow the cobwebs off love,' she said. 'Get it out of your system. I hope you do well. If you don't it doesn't matter. It's then start again time. Get yourself sorted . . .'

The following morning King rang Jock. 'Majestic? I've something to tell you.'

'See you at 12 as planned. Have you sharpened your pencil?'

'Balls,' laughed King. He was a new man.

Sitting in the luxury of the Majestic lounge the pair were close colleagues in adversity. Yet both felt a sense of freedom. 'Have you had any thoughts yet Jock?' asked King.

'Plenty. Most of them unprintable,' replied the Scotsman. 'I think I'm going to take a pub. I'll have enough to take a tenancy. I wouldn't be a manager for any bugger after what we've seen. At least it's something I know a bit about. I hope!'

Then Jock's face lit up. The first bitter of the day had sharpened his wits. 'I may have a bit of good news for you mate,' he said. 'A little matter of transport for your expedition, because you won't have the Sierra by then, they'll have tracked us down and taken them back. I've heard the recovery company are already rounding them up. In fact it might be a good idea for one of us to leave his car here in case we're pounced upon. We can always make some excuse about the wife just being out in it or something.'

'You're a convincing bugger, Jock. What's this transport you've got lined up for me, a camel?'

'Steady lad, don't look one in the mouth,' said Jock. 'Listen, I have a chum who has a caravette-camper thing. One of those that choke the Scottish Highland roads every summer. At the moment it's in mothballs for the winter.

'But for a small consideration he's willing to get it ready. He wants it to go to Brittany in June, so someone giving it a gentle run in would suit him. It's got everything Joe, sleeping, eating, cooking, washing, the lot.'

'Bloody hell, Jock. This sounds like the answer to the maiden's whatsit. You say a small consideration. What does that mean? I'm not on Fleet Street exes,' he joked.

'A bottle of Scotch a week should suffice. What do you think?'

'A bottle of Scotch? God, that's not a taxi fare these days.

Are you sure? 'It's a gift,' said King. 'Where does he live? Who is this bloke?'

'Just out of town. He's called Angus Ross. A retired fish manager from Aberdeen. Doesn't need the money. A lovely bloke. I'm surprised you haven't come across him in your travels.'

'I'm not a member of the golf club yet,' laughed King. 'And I don't suppose for a minute he uses the Roebuck. Give me his number.' The jigsaw was falling into place.

King had only one pint as he prepared his ideas for his interview with Keith Harris. 'Jock,' he said thoughtfully. 'You know the lakeland writer and walker Alfred Wainwright?'

'Who doesn't,' said Jock. 'He did all those wonderful guides to the mountains and the drawings and everything. You're not planning to be another Wainwright?'

'Don't be daft. But do you remember he also did a coast to coast walk from St Bees head on this side to Robin Hood's Bay on the Yorkshire coast.'

'I've got it at home,' said Jock.

'Well, my little idea is roughly to follow that.'

'What, over the bloody mountains?'

'No, but as near as I can get to it by road, taking in the same towns and villages. A coast to coast pub crawl. In Wainwright's footsteps.'

'Tyre marks,' retorted Jock. 'But it seems a fair idea. Give us a ring when you've see this bloke at the Press and if it's on I'll take you to meet Angus.'

King turned up at the Evening Press office and spoke to a smart looking lass on reception. 'Name's King,' he said. 'Joe King.' She looked at him sideways . . . but didn't say it.

'I'm here to see Keith Harris.'

'Do you have an appointment? Is he expecting you?'

'I bloody hope so,' said King. 'My whole future could depend on the next hour.'

The receptionist showed him to the lift. 'First floor, turn left. The news room's through the swing doors at the end. I'll give Keith a buzz and he'll be waiting for you.'

King did as he was told. The editorial floor was a drone of activity. A tall man in his early thirties with a shock of curly hair and a bit of a paunch walked down the office towards him and said, 'Joe King?'

'I am,' said King, taking an immediate liking to the lived-in face and the crinkles round Harris's eyes, obviously the inheritance of many hours of laughter.

'Come through,' said Harris. 'Let's have a chat.'

They sat at the news desk and the phone hardly stopped ringing. Harris said to a younger man sitting on his right, 'Take these calls for me, Willie.'

And he said to King: 'Now Joe! Tell me all about it. What's your idea?'

King explained how he was fed up with the life of a rep. How he'd developed a wanderlust and how he had been made redundant. He told Harris his idea about a cross country trip visiting pubs and describing life therein, the characters, the villages, the little northern towns. And he added: 'All I need is a bit of backing!'

'I like the idea,' said Harris. 'We are badly in need of a few new ideas around here,' he said glancing at his sidekick.

'If it's left to me there's a few quid in it plus expenses. I'll have to put it to the editor, of course. When could you start?'

'Say a week,' said King, groping desperately for a date – or guidance.

'Fine. And you say you'll have your own accommodation?'

'I've got to see a bloke about a caravette tonight,' said King.

'My God, we are keen,' said Harris. 'You've hardly been out of work a couple of days. In tonight? Good. I'll ring you at six when I've discussed it in this afternoon's news conference.'

King felt suddenly important. As if he had a mission in life. 'I thought news rooms were all clattering typewriters and reporters shouting "copy" when it had been submitted.'

'It's not like that now,' said Harris. 'Come on Joe, I'll show you round. The day of the typewriter has gone. It's all screens and keyboards. We can write with them, sub with them and even do page make-up and juggle stories around with them.

'The new intake into this profession will do well. The kids brought up on computer games and so on. For us who have been around a bit it's more difficult.'

They finished the tour back at the swing doors into editorial, and Harris shook King's hand. 'I think we've got a chance with this one. If the Old Man gives us the nod we'll have another get together and talk routes, deadlines and money. Remember Joe, deadlines are paramount. Even if you are out in the wilds, we'll want your stuff from the previous day on copy by 8.30am. So you'll have to write up the night before and line up a phone for the following morning.

'Remember all Post Offices don't open at 8.30. Remember phone boxes in villages may have the shit kicked out of them by yobboes the previous evening. Being on the road in this game requires organisation. Don't think it'll just be a jolly – if you know what I mean. I'll let you know if we've got the green light.'

Joe King walked out of the Press building in a bit of a daze and drove home. Maggie was waiting – still in the kitchen. 'How'd you get on Pet?' she asked.

'I should have a phone call by six. Jock's found me a caravette and I have to go and see this mate of his tonight and sort it out. If we get the go-ahead I could be on the road in a week or so. I'd better get the bloody atlas out.'

'You'd better get your car keys out,' said Maggie. 'I've had Cunliffe's transport manager on saying there are still a couple of company cars he can't trace.'

'Bugger. I need it still for a day or two. I'll go down the road and park it round the back of the Drunken Duck and clear it with Bert later. If they call, tell them my father's desperately ill in Barnsley or somewhere, and I've had to shoot off in it. Tell them I'll clear it as soon as I get back.'

'I don't know about a travel writer, you'll end up the wrong side of the press bench in court if you're not careful,' Maggie grinned. 'Go on, hide it. I'll cover for you. Be back for that phone call.'

'Don't worry kiddo,' said King. 'The whole of the rest of

our lives could depend on it.' He went and dumped the car and reported to Jock by phone. 'Six, they're ringing me Jock,' he said. 'When I know more I'll give you a bell and we'll go and see your Angus Ross. I'll meet you downtown at 7.30. Have you given him a ring yet?'

'I have,' said Jock. 'He's happy with the arrangement. Says it needs a good run anyway. There's no problem with the insurance – but obviously he wants to have a look at you. He doesn't want some big dirty itinerant and his family on a jaunt across England in it. I've told him you're half civil and we'll see him tonight.'

'Thanks mate,' said King, and rang off.

The phone rang before six, and King jumped to his feet. 'Joe, Keith Harris here. The boss says OK. Come and see me tomorrow lunchtime. We'll have a spot of lunch and set things into action. Looking forward to it? Just do us a bloody good job, man,' Harris said and rang off.

King left his car behind the Dirty Duck and was picked up by Jock.

'You'll find Ross a funny old so and so,' said the Scotsman. 'He's a hard bitten old sod who worked a long time in Africa. He still likes to go back and see his chums. He had some government post, but finds it hard to get away from Annie these days. She always finds him a job to do now he's retired. That's why he wants the van ready to take her off to France in a couple of months. And while you're running it in on your barmy scheme, he's hoping to nip off to Durban for a couple of weeks. Let's go and see him.'

Angus Ross lived in the posh suburbs. He had a front drive with trees and a chain-link fence across the front of his lawn. 'Jeez, Jock, if this is what the overseas service gets you, put me down for some,' said King.

The man who answered the door was wiry, short and had a thin nose. He sported a salt and pepper moustache, wore a cravat under his white shirt. And he looked military.

'What-ho Henderson,' he said to Jock. 'Nice to see you again man. So this is your pal?'

Jock introduced them in the broad hall of the house. 'Come in and have a dram,' he said, leading the couple into a comfortable lounge, warmed by a roaring fire, and pouring liberal measures of Famous Grouse into crystal whisky glasses.

'So you're off a-travelling Mr King,' he said. 'I'll show you the van when it's light in the morning. It's got just about everything you'll need for a trip across the north. It's pretty cosy.'

A woman's voice with the strong Scottish accent called from the kitchen. 'Whatever you're up to Angus, you're not going to Africa until you've finished that wall.'

King and Jock looked at each other. Ross laughed. 'See what I'm up against? I arranged to go off and see my old chums and she got me to build a bloody wall round the bottom flower bed. And look at my hands,' he laughed showing gnarled fingers. Two days, that's all it'll take me and then I'm off like a Zulu's assegai.

'Call round about 10 in the morning and I'll unlock the van for you and show you what's what.' He showed them the door and they left.

'He's certainly got a way with him, the old sod,' said King. 'But I'm grateful mate. Come round for the christening and we'll dunk it's head in a drop of Scotch.'

The pair parted and King went in to report to Maggie. '. . . and she actually said, "You're not going to Africa till you've finished that wall",' said King, chortling as he turned off the light.

6

King collected his hidden company car from behind the Duck at twenty to ten and parked at one minute to outside Ross's house. He looked like a punctual man – even if he couldn't get to Africa just when he wanted to.

The old boy was in the garden and headed straight for the smart-looking green and cream caravette. 'I've been over it. Everything's working, the fridge, the stove – even the bloody engine,' he chuckled. 'The lav works but you'll have to bring your own bedding. All it needs is petrol and a large bottle of calor gas. And you're on your way man. Good luck.'

King couldn't believe his luck. The vehicle was three years but looked like new. 'Look, I can't accept this for a bottle of Scotch a week,' said King. 'I'll make it two.'

Ross grinned. 'Okay. Just look after it. Run it in gently. Don't get pissed when you're driving and bring it back clean. That's all I ask. Here's the keys, collect it when you want it. This morning's fine by me. One month is it? Good luck man,' he said, and went off to finish his wall so he could go to Africa.

King went home and told Maggie the scene. 'It's incredible,' he said. 'I'll give Jock a ring so he can run me over to collect it. I'll bring it back here and then I've got that lunch with Keith Harris.'

'You sound like Ian Wooldridge off on his travels again,' grinned Alison. 'Just get on Daily Mail money mate – or get it out of your system.'

King grinned: 'King of the road, that's me. I feel like a bloody superstar already. I'm off to see Harris. Look love, you start your new job on Monday. I'm going to leave on Sunday and get up there.'

'Then call in Smith's and get yourself a couple of maps. You're not exactly Marco Polo at the best of times.' King laughed and left to see the news editor.

Harris took him to, of all places, the Majestic for lunch. King was greeted affably by Don the barman. Harris commented: 'You seem fairly well known in here!'

'Oh, I come in now and again with a colleague,' said King. 'Friendly place.'

Harris did them royally. Pate, duck à l'orange and cheese, accompanied by a bottle of decent claret.

'So when can you start, Joe?' he asked.

'Monday,' said King.

'Okay, we'll blurb it on Monday and you file your first piece on Tuesday at eight thirty, okay? When we leave here come back to the office and we'll get the snappers to take a picture of you for your by-line and the art department to do us a couple of logos which we can use each time we carry your stuff. Don't forget you're new at the game. We'll carry it every two days for the first week and see how it goes from there. About 500 words each piece, okay?'

King's head was reeling. Most of this was new language to him. 'Sure,' he said, with more confidence than he felt, 'I'll talk to you each morning Keith, and after I've put my stuff over. How's that?'

'You're getting the hang of it,' said Harris. 'Go for it. Remember, I'm just a phone call away!'

'Bloody hell, Jock,' said King to his pal when he called to pick him up to get the caravette. 'I hope I know what I'm doing. It's a bit of a risk you know.'

'As the man said, go for it pal,' said Jock. 'Let's get your gypsy caravan and get you organised. Thought of food?'

'Not really,' said King. 'There's plenty of fish and chip shops up there.'

'For breakfast? Don't be bloody daft wee man. Let's get you stocked up.'

The pair raided the hypermarket shelves. Soups, baked beans, corned beef, tea bags, bacon, eggs, three six packs of lager. The usual stuff.

'Got your disprins!' grinned Jock.

'Bollocks,' answered King. 'And I can get bread, fruit, milk and all the fresh things when I get up there.'

'Here we go mate. Why worry about money when your father's got piles!'

A voice from the next table in the lounge of the Majestic boomed out like the noise from a rag-gatherer's trumpet: 'We'll have less of that talk here, thank you.'

'And up yours too missus,' said King as they left. 'I'm off on my adventures.'

Don, the barman laughed: 'Want to borrow my compass and dividers?'

'And the same to you mate,' said King as he left with Jock to make his final preparations. 'You'd think he was Scott of the bloody Antarctic,' said Don, serving the colonel with a pink gin. 'He's only going to Cumberland, for God's sake.'

The weekend flashed by and on Sunday King said a sad goodbye to Maggie and the kids. 'Bon voyage chuck,' she said, wiping her eyes.

'And you with your job, love,' said King. 'I'll ring you tonight. It's fingers crossed time.'

And he drove off in his caravette to start the greatest adventure of his life. The motorway traffic was lighter than his heart. What, he asked himself, the bloody hell have I got myself into?

Stocked up, a full tank, maps and guides and an assurance of a few bob from the Evening Press. What more could he want? I want to get this over, he told himself.

It was late Easter, and the holiday traffic hadn't started. But the rain had got going early. And the wind. And the waves. The ones that had dodged Ireland and the Isle of Man beat against the base of the cliffs. I wonder, said King to himself, if it was like this when old Wainwright set off? At least I've got shelter.

It was going dark when he found the caravan site. It was desolate, late afternoon and cheerless. King parked up, and tested the facilities by making himself a cup of tea and a corned beef sandwich. He donned his anorak and went for a walk. It was not exactly Costa del Sol. The gift shops were closed and the few traders were thinking about following suit. He bought a stick of rock in the paper shop just for the sake of it. A reminder of the start of his great adventure.

He didn't find much to look at and the west wind was shaping his trousers round the mould of his legs. The two pubs he passed were making a meal of rattling the bolts as they stuttered into life for the Sunday evening. They didn't look inviting. King realised he should have set up camp at St Bees Head. He was considering heading back for his camper and moving on when he came upon a corner with friendly lights, a white hotel and he saw through the leaded light windows a fire burning in the grate and a bunch of blokes round the bar. He went in.

King ordered a half of lager and sat in the corner, taking in the atmosphere. A big round face under a ratting cap and looking over a heavy overcoat weighed him up 'Travelling?' he asked.

'Just a few days off,' said King, giving nothing away. 'Having a ride around.'

'Staying round here?' he was asked.

'Oh! Just overnight,' said King, fingering the spiral back of his notebook in his pocket.

'Some funny buggers round here,' said his companion. 'Lot of rogues. Watch them or they'll have you. Always up to japes, they are,' said the unsure local. 'What do they call you mate?'

'All sorts of things,' said King. 'But I'm Joe King.' As soon as he said it he regretted it.

'You what?'

'Don't even think of saying it,' said King.

The cap and overall looked into his pint pensively for a few seconds and thought better of it. 'I'm Sam Nugent,' he said. 'How-do.'

The pair were unconsciously mentally boxing when a florid-faced heavyweight walked over to the fire to warm his backside, belching loudly as he settled.

'Early for the corncrake,' commented Sam, his face never showing a flicker of a smile.

King thought: 'There's going to be some colourful stuff up here, but I can't file stories about blokes with flatulence.'

The natives had ordered food. There was a good smell of beef pie, and sparks were flying off the knives and forks. King ordered some off a barmaid who looked to have too many teeth. She had more trouble closing her mouth than some members of the royal household. To say she looked horsey was putting it mildly.

He took his place back at the table when his number was called. It was rather like winning a Christmas draw. 'And next on the blue ticket, number 19, beef pie and chips.' But it was wholesome and tasty.

'He'll fart in a minute,' said Sam unexpectedly, nodding towards Windy Walter, still warming the whole of his body in front of the fire.

'Oh,' said King, caught completely on the wrong foot. What do you say to that?

And with no further ado the fire hogger eased himself forward with a satisfied smile and broke wind loudly. 'Oops,' he said. 'I've dropped something I can't pick up,' and took another swig.

'He always says that,' said Sam. 'He's right dirty, dopey bugger. When he came to live here about five years ago he told everyone he was an ostrich salesman. Took a council house, he did. It only had a small back yard and people used to walk past to see if he'd got any ostriches. When they asked him he'd tell them it was a thin time, and he hadn't come across any yet. Ostriches! He couldn't deal in bloody blackbirds. I reckon he's on the run from a home for the confused. Bloody ostriches . . .'

King was chortling. He'd been on the scene less than an hour and he'd already found an ostrich salesman. In Cumbria! There must be something there for his first piece.

He waited for the flatulent bum warmer to go to the bar and joined him.

'Still cold,' he said.

'Aye.'

'I'm just having a ride around between jobs. Lot of people out of work at the moment,' said King, trying to promote some sort of rapport.

'Aye.'

'You working?' asked King, more in hope than expectation.

'Aye. I sell ostriches.'

'Must be few and far between up here,' said King.

'Aye. But I advertised and I've got a lot of orders.'

'Where do you get them? The ostriches, not the orders.'

'Africa.'

'Not building a wall are you?' asked King.

The ostrich salesman looked at him. 'Are you bloody barmy, or what?' he asked King. King left. As he walked towards the caravan park he was forming a piece for the Press in his mind. And he still had 24 hours to get it all together. Things were looking promising.

He stopped off to phone Maggie from a box. 'I'm here, fed and watered and I'm going for an early night,' he told her.

'Oh yeah!' she joked. 'Come across any scoops, yet?'

'Just an ostrich salesman who farts a lot,' said King.

'Must be good ale up there, Joe,' she said. 'Straight to bed now. Give us a shout tomorrow night.'

King let himself into the warm van. The calor heater had done its job. He brewed himself a tea bag, had a brief wash and brush up and settled himself into his bunk with an Ordnance Survey sheet and Wainwright's coast to coast book.

Hell fire, he thought. Life on the open road. No Roebuck tomorrow morning. And no bloody Evans. Life had a different look to it already.

Tomorrow he would go through the village of Cleator Moor

and branch off to have a look at Ennerdale Water. His first lake. His first full day in action as the Evening Press's northern rover. The possibilities were endless. He went to sleep with a smile on his face.

7

Joseph King awoke to a spring morning. February had filled the dikes, the March wind seemed to have blown itself out and the April rains were still packing their bags for their annual assault on humanity.

Outside the birds were singing. The sparrows were pecking at the moss, preparing material for their next housing estate in the hedges, trees and eaves. Last night's angry sea had cooled its temper and settled into a more friendly swell. And by the time the bacon was grilling, the eggs sizzling and the tea in the pot things were looking like heaven for a man whose life, just weeks ago, had been stamped: 'Sentenced to Drudgery.'

He thought of last night's encounters. The farter and Sam's comments. He opened the van door and bellowed, in a surge of happy release: 'Early for the corncrake.' A woman returning to her trailer having taken her spaniel for its morning ablutions just happened to be passing. In all her years of caravanning on this site she had never been so startled. She looked at King, took a firmer grip on the lead, and legged it back to her accommodation. As King drove off he saw her and her partner, who wore a woolly cardigan with a zip and a fold-over collar, peering curiously at him through the rear window of their van.

King waved cheerily and they both ducked out of sight. Suburban curtain twitchers, thought King, laughing his way onto the main road. Here we go, here we go, here we go!

He stopped at the first village to phone Harris at the Press. 'Well, you got there Joe,' said the editor. 'Any ideas?'

'Well, I'm just leaving, but I've come across a farting ostrich salesman.'

'Oh yes,' said Harris. It's not something there's really any answer to. 'Can you weave it into tomorrow's piece?'

'Easy,' said King. 'But I don't suppose I can say "fart".'

'Ways round it,' laughed Harris. 'Use "wind" or "flatulence". But don't worry about vocabulary or the syntax. Leave that to the subs. Have a good day. Five hundred words at eight thirty in the morning, ok?'

'Sure,' said King. 'See you Keith.' His words masked his nervousness.

He headed inland, and the road seemed lonely. Where now? The lanes seemed too narrow for his van and he found the winding road to Ennerdale led nowhere – except to Ennerdale, the most north westerly of the lakes, a shining level dwarfed by high crags and lower mountains, their heads still covered like dandruff.

The south side is for quiet people. The north side for campers and walkers. King wanted none of these. He wanted 500 words of fun and chatter. He wasn't going to get it here, as beautiful as the scenery was. He felt mildly irritated that he had to retrace his journey to get back on the beaten track and find life.

All the villages seemed deserted, but he decided not to panic. Then he hit the jackpot. A lakeside village with two pubs and a hotel. And it was almost noon. This surely had to be worth putting in another silver dollar and pulling the handle. Have a go, Joe . . .

He parked up in the area reserved for such vehicles as his and went into the first pub. He ordered a half and sat in the corner with his paper. Then it walked in.

Out of the hefty brown brogues sprouted plus fours, a country-style check woollen shirt as favoured at game fairs, a brown hacking jacket, all topped by a large grey moustache, a florid face and the traditional farmer's cap, which, at least, he had the grace to remove as he entered.

'Pint of your best bitter please, landlord,' he said to the publican.

'Certainly, sir. Thrapes or Girlings?'

'Like the traditional,' he boomed. 'But whatever will be,

will be, that's what I always say. At this moment in time I feel in favour of the Thrapes. What's the specific gravity?'

The landlord, glancing in my direction, as if in need of help, told him.

The landlord told him, standing like an expectant beggar with the empty pint glass in his hand.

'Well, that's not the be all and end all, is it?' said pain-in-the-arse. 'The bottom line in the flavour – and the effect, what? When I'm out and about I leave no stone unturned to find a new brew which suits my palate. Just had one up the road, but no names, no pack drill. But I must say you've got me on the horns of a dilemma.'

King already had his notebook out and was scribbling swift jottings.

The blusterer finally made up his mind and the landlord took his money fast and vanished to the other bar.

That was the stuff he was looking for, and King was just finished his notes – oh, for shorthand – when two locals, obviously farm workers entered the bar.

King heard one say to his mate: 'Oh God, it's him again.'

Blustering Bill spotted them straight away. 'Ah, I'm on my travels again.' he said loudly.

'So I see,' said one, with a shock of dusty hair and large mucky boots. 'Been far?'

'Every pub from here to Lancaster, what, what?'

'Oh aye, well we're grafting, so we'll leave you to it.'

'Grafting eh? Many hands make light work, what?'

'I prefer to think too many cooks spoil the broth,' said the farm labourer with a flash of genius. 'Come on Lol, we'll have a game of pool.'

The plaid and moustache looked at me: 'Salt of the earth, what? Must go old boy, the dog'll be eating the chops in the car. Must get on with my tour. Remember, it's a long road that had no turning.'

'Well,' said King, 'You should find it a short route round here. I haven't found a 100-yard straight yet.'

King finished his half and left. That, he thought to himself with satisfaction, will help no end.

On the road to Rosthwaite he toyed with the idea of having a look at Seathwaite, the wettest place in England. But it was such a lovely day he didn't risk it and carried on to Keswick, a handsome old market town with a warren of pubs and, no doubt a hive of busy bollocked characters and comics. He parked for the night. Enough was enough anyway, in the van he was not used to among the winding lanes. On several occasions he'd thought he was going to scrape the jutting stone walls as ungentlemanly cars flashed by in the other direction.

Why, he wondered to himself, is it always me to give way to these bastards?

As he wandered along Keswick's old main street with its ancient market hall in the middle of the road, a thought struck him. He'd done the coast to Keswick in one fell swoop.

He decided to stay where he was for a couple of days and do a bit of ferreting about. The public bar at the Bale of Hay was buzzing with late lunchtime drinkers. Local layabouts, tourists, shopkeepers – a fair kaleidoscope of life. 'Pint of lager and a round of ham and pickle, please,' King ordered from an attractive dark-haired, dark-eyed lass behind the bar.

She served him and said pleasantly: 'Passing through?'

'Stopping over a couple of nights,' said King.

'On holiday?'

'No, a redundant brewery rep having a look how the other half live.'

'Where are you staying? Over at the hotel?'

'No such luck. I've got a camper parked up on the caravan park. I'm doing a bit of research work on life this side of the bar for the local paper.'

'What, for publishing?'

'I bloody hope so,' said King. 'I'm looking for a few characters to chat to. What's your name?'

'Well, they call me all sorts of things in here. But it says Molly on the certificate. And you?'

'I'm Joe King,' said King waiting for it.

'You bloody must be,' said Molly. But her grin was friendly.

'Give me a shout if you want anything.' King wasn't sure if he'd been given the glad eye. There was certainly a hint of something in her wink.

He sat in the corner, drawn by the click of the dominoes and the warmth of the fire, listening to the crack of the locals. This, he thought, is why there's no place like an English pub. They've tried in the United States, but got nowhere near it – except on television. And that's script-written. This was all off the cuff.

A lovely local accent said: 'And that double five had all you buggers knocking. Game,' he said with satisfaction as he placed the last five at the far end of the crocodile of dominoes that stretched across the table. They all pushed 10p towards him from their piles of varying sizes. 'You're a jammy sod, Jed,' laughed one.

Jed looked towards the door as his mate shuffled for the next hand. 'Watch your pockets, here's Mahatma Coat,' he said.

They all looked over to the bar where an Asian stood and ordered a whisky.

King scribbled 'Mahatma Coat,' in his book. He was quite looking forward to completing his first piece.

Jed looked at him: 'Not from round these parts are you mate?'

'No,' said King. 'Just doing a bit of research for an article.'

Jed laughed. 'Well, you've come to the right bloody place. Take old Mahatma there. He has a second hand shop and pleads poverty. But look at him, he's got more gold in his teeth than Tutankamen. Bastards! Should stay in their bazaars back home. But I guess they can't stand the poverty. So they come and rook us. And we're daft enough to feed 'em. Some of them live 10 to a house and 3 to a bed! Mind, if the mix was right, that might not be bad,' he grinned.

'Come on, Jed,' said his mate. 'Your drop.'

Jed laid double six and called to the Indian at the bar: 'Had a good morning Mahatma? Do we still own Helvellyn and Windermere or have you flogged them to the Arabs? Cheating bugger.'

The Indian took it well. He had little option. Rubbing his hands he looked at Jed and smiled: 'I am thinking you are funny man. Perhaps I can sell you something if you come in. It will not be a mountain or a lake, but I have acquired very good set of Victorian toys. You seem to like games. Perhaps you would like some marbles.'

'No thanks, mate, I've got all mine,' was the quick reply. 'I suppose you gave five quid for them and want five hundred?'

The Indian smiled. 'Every man has a right to make a living,' he said, spreading his hands in the age old way of dishonest dealers.

'Do you have any old carpets?' asked Jed. His three companions looked at him as if he'd gone mad.

'Oh! Very good Turkish carpets,' said Mahatma, rubbing his hands.

'Then get yourself a magic one and piss off home.' The bar crackled with laughter. 'Right lads, where were we?' said my new chum as the game carried on and the Indian went back to his back street shop. King decided he'd go find him in the morning.

Jed won the next hand too and then turned to King. 'If you're looking for some local colour come here tonight about eight. The back bar. It's Karaoke night. You've never seen so many Elvis Presley's and Frank Sinatras.'

King went for a refill and Molly gave him a big smile. 'You seem to be settling in with the locals.'

'Just had a good laugh at the business with the Indian. Was he upset?'

'Upset? The bugger comes in every day. He gets some like that every day. He loves it. I guess he knows deep down he's smarter than this lot, and he comes in to wind them up.'

'Rum part of the world this,' said King to the barmaid. 'Where you from?'

'Yorkshire. So near yet so far. Different folks, different humour. But there's a lot of fun goes on in here.'

'I've noticed,' said King. 'And I understand there's going to be more fun tonight.'

'Aye, music night. You've seen nowt like it. Four or five pints and they all think they're on the verge of the big time. You coming?'

'I sure am. But I can't be that late, I've some writing to do before I turn in.'

'See you tonight then,' said Molly, leaving to answer the summons from the bar bell in the snug.

This, thought King, is turning out to be quite promising.

It was with regret he left the ambience of the Bale of Hay. 'See you tonight,' he called to the dominoes table. Jed and his mates looked up. 'Aye, hope you know bloody My Way.'

King went back to have a brew and write up some notes – get a few ideas on paper. He'd top it up later tonight when he got back from the Kareoke night. He hoped.

He had a quick kip, a shower and changed. He didn't have his Elvis suit handy, but he didn't plan on doing a stage act. At eight o'clock he locked the van and headed for the pub, bright eyed and bushy tailed. Pen and pad in his anorak pocket. He still needed a bit more for his first 500 words.

Jolly Molly spotted him as soon as he entered. 'Pint, Joe?' she asked.

'Please love,' he said. 'By gum, it gets going early doesn't it?' The public bar where he'd spent lunchtime was comfortably full, the fire still roaring up the chimney. Jed and his pals were still playing dominoes. 'Have they been here all day?' King asked Molly.

'Oh, no, they're just early starters. They're all either retired or out of work – or don't want to work, wink, wink,' laughed Molly.

'You'd think they were playing for the town hall clock, but I'll bet there's not 50p in it at the end of the night. And it evens itself out over the week. They only stray from the normal on Thursdays when they have rum chasers. Thursday is benefit day, dole day, call it what you like. It all comes out of the same pot.'

The would-be stage artists were already under way in the back room, singing to piped music from the machine.

'You want to go through if you want a laugh, Joe,' said Molly. 'It's an education.'

King took a swig of his pint and wandered through. It was a typical lakeland town pub, the walls stained dark brown in tobacco smoke. He entered the club room, as they called it, to be greeted with a wonderful sight. An old boy of about 60, an open-necked shirt and bright red braces accentuating an enormous stomach, was in full flow at the microphone. The buttons of his shirt were fighting to keep the beer gut in place.

He was giving vent to an old fifties number 'Hang down your head, Tom Dooley'. But every time that particular line came up, the local lads drowned him out with: 'Hang down your leg, long tooley', and roared self approval each time they achieved it.

This was too good to miss. King took a seat in the corner and in no time found himself joining in – with both the rude line and the infectious laughter.

Fat Belly Jones went on to Rose Marie, trying to emulate Slim Whitman and getting nowhere near. He rounded his act off with 'The pub with no beer'.

Next came a lass of about 20 in jeans and a tight sweater who gave voice to an old medley, including 'Bobby's Girl' and 'Love Letters in the Sand', before going all modern and wailing a Whitney Houston number, and doing quite as well as Barbara Streisand!

The beer flowed, the smoke thickened and the laughter got louder. There didn't seem to be any prize at the end of the night. 'Jailhouse Rock and Heartbreak Hotel' had had several airings. A lot of drink had been consumed. Most of them could handle it, but three youths who had gone the full session left with their arms round each other for support.

He was behind them as they reached the public bar. The players were just putting the dominoes back in the box as they staggered past their table. 'There they go,' said Jed. 'Their heads are dangling like Christmas turkeys on a market stall. They'll feel great in the morning!'

He put his pot on the bar and Molly smiled: 'Quickie for the road?'

'I shouldn't really. I've to write up to be ready to phone it over first thing in the morning. But go on then . . .'

King asked where was the nearest pay phone to the caravan site. 'Which one are you on?' said Molly.

'Larchfield,' said King.

'You can use mine if you want. I live just round the corner. That's Caunce Street. Number three. It's the bottom flat.'

'That'd be a help,' said King. 'But I'll be early – about eight fifteen.'

'That's not early for me,' said Molly. 'I have to do my jobs early to be here for ten thirty to bottle up.'

'Thanks a lot,' said King, draining his last half. 'See you in the morning.'

He returned to his base, got out his new parcel of 500 sheets of foolscap and put pen to paper.

By the time he'd screwed up and discarded several sheets he was happy with his first effort – and was surprised to find he had exceeded his words order. He'd given them the lot: The crashing waves, the tinkling streams, the snow-capped fells. Witty Sam, the flatulent bum-warmer, blustering Bill, the man who spoke in clichés, Mahatma Coat, the pies, the laughs, the dominoes and Jolly Molly.

He had so much to go at he decided to leave Kareoake night until his next piece. He didn't have to name all the pubs anyway, just the town or area. King guessed that was something to do with libel.

He slept like a child, waking early and taking a moment or two to get his bearings. He had a cup of tea and a shower before going to find Caunce Street, which was only 200 yards away. It had tidy terraced houses on each side of the road. They looked as if people had pride in their little properties. He was bang on time as he knocked on Molly's door. She opened it wearing a floral housecoat and a smile.

'By heck, you're punctual,' she said.

'You know what it is when you've got a deadline to meet.'

52

grinned King. He got through to the Press on a transfer call and asked for copy. A cheerful voice answered immediately. 'Hi Joe, I've been briefed by Keith about what you're doing and that you're not used to putting copy over. Don't worry about it love. Just give it me in clauses at your own pace. I'll put in the punctuation – as long as you tell me what's in quotes. OK.'

Joe stumbled through his first piece, and the taker said: 'Right, I've to put this down and I'll put you through to Keith. Hang on.' When he got through to the desk in a couple of minutes, Harris told him: 'Good stuff Joe. Keep up the anecdotes rather than the travelogue stuff. I like the "Corncrake" and the domino players and the cliché man. We're using this tonight. If it doesn't all get in don't worry, we've got a small paper tonight and the leader of the council has been found dead in peculiar circumstances. These things happen. But it'll get a show. Ring me in the morning and tell me were you are. Next piece Thursday – same time.'

When King replaced the receiver he was surprised to see his hands were shaking. An old hack would put over 500 words off the top of his head, making it up as he went along. Your first piece is a bit more worrying. But he'd done it.

He went through to the kitchen to thank Molly and she offered him a steaming mug of coffee. 'Pop in any time you're passing,' she said. 'Are you coming into the Bale at lunchtime?'

'For half an hour,' he said. 'Where does Mahatma Coat hang out?'

'Arkwright Street, behind the pub. You going to see him?'

'I think so. He should have some tales to tell. The only thing is I can't be seen to be here for another night. I'm supposed to be on my travels.'

'Go and see him. He's got another place in Ambleside. You can catch up with him again later. He's got a tale to tell all right. He's supposed to be a descendant of the Raj. The son of a nobleman.'

'What, selling rubbish in back streets?'

'Finish your coffee. I'm going in early. I'll show you where he hangs out.'

Mahatma's shop was an unholy muddle, from the stuff in the window to the packed inside which was like an assault course. A little bell tinkled over the door. Mahatma appeared through a curtain of beaded strings at the back, rubbing his hands hopefully. He'd never had a customer this early.

'What can I be doing for you,' he smiled hopefully.

'Well, I'm all right for marbles,' grinned King. 'I'm looking for a story.'

'Story? I have many good books, some very old.'

'No, you've got it wrong. I don't want to buy a book, I want you to give me a story.'

The smile evaporated off Mahatma's face. 'What is this givings?' he asked in confusion. 'I am businessman, not here for givings.'

King explained: 'Look, I'm from the Evening Press. I'm going across the country looking for characters and writing about them. If we do one on you, think of the free advertising it'll mean.'

Mathatma's eyes began to uncloud. 'You mean free advertising for my shops?' he asked. 'What can I be doing for you my friend?'

'Well, there can't be that many Indian second hand dealers in the Lake District. I understand you are from a high family. I first noticed you in the pub yesterday lunchtime. You were having some fun with the locals.'

'You mean they were having fun with me. They call me Mahatma Coat. That is quite funny. But I always hit back. It is give one, take one. My name is Mahatma Sidhu.'

King took out his notebook and began to scribble. 'And where, exactly are you from?'

'The west, near to Bombay in a very beautiful area. In the days of the Empire we were thriving, but many things go sour.

'Politics and fighting took over and my father lost, how you say, his dynasty. It is decided to bring the family to England. Most stay in London and Birmingham, but I like to breathe the air like home.'

'What was your father?' asked King.

'He was a prince. Not a high prince, just a medium prince.'

'Bloody hell,' exclaimed King. 'So you are a prince too?'

'In a manner of speaking. I was son of prince when things broke up.'

'And you also have a business in Ambleside?'

'Like this. When you are there, you see.'

I can't do two pieces from one place. May I see you in Ambleside tomorrow?'

'My goodness me,' said Mahatma. 'I am up the hill away from the lake. In the old town. This is my address.' He wrote it down and King said: 'I'll see you tomorrow. If it's lunchtime, where will you be?'

'There is a very fine hostelry next door. I am either in the emporium or in there. They call me Mahatma Coat there too. But I take their money.'

King left with a spring in his step. He could see it now. 'The second hand dealer they call Mahatma Coat in his Lakeland local is, unbeknown to the mickey takers, an Indian Prince . . .'

Not a bad start to the day. He bought another stick of rock, a postcard for Jock, had a look round the better antique shops, winced at the prices and left, and strolled into the Bale.

Molly was just putting the cobs into the glass case – the usual imaginative beef, ham or cheese, and Jed and his chums were just settling, the wooden dominoes box still unopened on the scrubbed table.

He smiled at Molly and said: 'Thanks for the phone.'

And Jed's dulcet tones pierced across the bar: 'Here he is, Trevor McDonald, News at Ten, Keswick.'

They didn't hang around, this lot. King grinned at them and took it good humouredly. 'I'll get you some new dominoes from Mathatma's – well second hand ones anyway.'

'Why's that?' asked Jed. 'You've almost rubbed the bloody spots off those.' He in turned grinned. 'One a piece at half time,' he conceded. 'You're leaving today.'

'Yeah. But I might be back. At this rate I'll have my mission accomplished well inside the time limit and I'd like another couple of days round here before I join the dole queue.'

'So you're coming to see me again,' said Molly, her eyes smiling.

'I think I might just do that,' said King. 'Let's get the business over first.'

He drank his half slowly and said what he was surprised to find was a rather sad farewell. He patted Molly on the arm and said: 'See you.'

He nodded to the dominoes players as he left, and Jed shouted: 'Good luck lad. You turn right for Ambleside. If you turn left you'll be in bloody Scotland.' He could hear them laughing as he left the bar.

There is, in fact, only one road between Keswick and Ambleside. He was glad to see the huge mass of Helvellyn was still on the left. Mahatma hadn't sold it. And he decided to stop off at Grasmere for lunch. Like Rosthwaite, this was right on Wainwright's route. It deserved a historical ferret around anyway.

It was still spring like as he pulled into the huge car park, ignoring the good sheepskin and woollen shops. He wandered into the church yard to have a quick peek at old Wordsworth's grave and bought some gingerbread in the centuries old corner shop that used to be the village school. He bought more rock for the kids and put his stuff in the van, collecting his notebook and strolled into the village centre.

Not fancying one of the grander hotels that would have sucked away a fair portion of his resources, he headed for the little black and white Lamb's Head.

The most fun is always to be found in the public bar, and that's where he settled. And he couldn't believe his eyes. He groaned inwardly. There, holding forth at the bar was the Cliché King. He thought he'd have been in Lancaster by now.

'Well, as I always say, people in glass houses shouldn't throw stones. It's just the thin end of the wedge, what? And remember, you can't put all your eggs in one basket.'

Nobody was taking any notice of him at all. He was dressed exactly as he had been yesterday. 'Ah, well,' he said, finishing his pint of very best bitter, 'can't be hanging around in pubs all day, can we? Least said, soonest mended.'

Nobody moved. He left, and the half dozen locals let off a sigh of relief.

'Somebody's going to do something to him one day,' said an old farmer type. 'I think we're going to have to set one up for him before long.'

King ordered a half and a beef sandwich. They'd run out of mustard.

The locals were chatting, King almost missed the click of the dominoes. 'Having another Bert?' said the farmer. 'Hellfire, that was funny last night. Never seen owt like it,' said Bert. 'You weren't here, were you Jim?'

'No,' said a little ferret-faced man with dark hair. 'What happened?'

'You know we were playing the Creaking Gate at darts?'

'Aye, we were thrashing them and their captain tried to say Bert's treble twenty was in treble five. He was shouted down and they lost the match. He's such a good loser he grabbed the plate of sandwiches and swatt 'em on back of t' fire.' He pronounced swatt like fat.

'Gerrout,' laughed Jim. 'Always thought he was a funny bugger. What happened?'

'Well, there was a lot of shoving and pushing, and for a moment it looked like turning into something for a John Wayne picture. But it settled when Sergeant Blake walked in, off duty like, for a pint. Brilliant, he was. Never said a word, though he obviously knew something was askew. The return match against them should be fun.'

Bert noticed King smiling to himself at the bar.

'Stranger?' he asked, knowing full well he was. 'There's some funny happenings in these hills, I can tell you. Bit early for your holidays aren't you?'

'Working.' said King. 'Doing a few pieces for the Evening Press. That sounds like a rum do last night.'

'Eh, don't be putting that in your paper,' said Jim.

'Hang on,' said Bert. 'Let's get the bugger back. Teach

him to chuck us suppers onto back of fire.'

'There's always been ill-feeling between us and the Gate,' he said. 'But this was the best yet. Talk about bad losers . . .' He told King the full story.

He repeated the tale, which improved with telling. It ended with angry mutterings and threats from both sides. The presence of Sergeant Blake had saved the situation. But it was obviously far from over.

'Where's the Gate?' asked King, knowing he'd have to get the other side of the story if he was to get it in the paper.

'Ambleside,' said Bert. 'Back Street, near the car park. Supposed to be a mecca for tourists peering behind the scenes in the Lakes and for drinkers of real ale – you know, those soft buggers who hold their pint to the light and say it's cloudy.

'They'd do better looking behind the kitchen door at the grease and asking where the brew comes from. The locals say the other end of the mild line is in the beck. Bastard. We wouldn't go for the return match except we'd be labelled mardy buggers in the town.'

'Let's take them on at kick boxing instead,' said Jim.

'Kick boxing? You couldn't kick a habit,' laughed Bert. 'But I reckon that Alfie Whelan should be in an institute for the silly.'

King asked: 'He's the captain? The bloke who started it?'

'Aye, that's him. A right nasty sod. There was trouble last season when one of Whelan's lot threw up outside and came back to tell our landlord Terry it was the only ale that tasted better coming up that it did going down.'

'Almost got a clouting for that,' said Jim.

'Is Terry in?' asked King. 'I'd like a word with him.'

'Cash and carry,' said Bert. 'He'll be back in a few minutes.'

When Terry Williamson appeared, King took an instant liking to the broad Cumbrian, who told him: 'We don't want that lot down here again. But what can you do? There're in the league and we have to play them twice. There's a few who'll be voting them out the annual meeting in June. Nobody likes them.'

'Can I quote you on any of that?' asked King.

'Just say we HAVE to play them – after that no comment.'

King arrived in Ambleside in mid-afternoon and settled in. He posted Jock's card and one to the kids. With time to spare he took a walk, found the Creaking Gate and Mahatma's shop for tomorrow. He cooked himself some bacon and eggs and Cumberland sausages.

At six he rang Maggie. She was enjoying her new job. The kids were fine. Cunliffe's Brewery were still looking for his office car. Maggie was missing him. Had he seen tonight's paper with his picture by-line and first piece on the feature page.

He asked her to save them for him as he wouldn't be able to get a copy at all his ports of call.

He went into the Gate early doors. It was empty. The man behind the door looked as if his bum itched and he suffered from halitosis. King ordered a Scotch, not wishing to risk the beck water. After a couple of minutes tittle tattle, he ventured: 'I'm from the Evening Press. We've had a call about a bit of a shindig at Grasmere last night over a game of darts. Understand you were involved.'

'They're cheating buggers,' said Whelan, looking as if he didn't want to discuss the matter. 'They tried to say 15 was 60. We don't fall for tricks like that.'

'They say it's you who are the baddies,' said King. 'They say you don't have a very sporting reputation.'

'They would,' said Whelan. 'We always have trouble up there. We'll do 'em one day.'

'Do you want to play the return?' asked King.

'No, but they won't get any bloody sandwiches.'

'Well, they won't be able to throw them on the fire,' said King. 'That wasn't too sporting.'

'You've been talking to them,' said Whelan. 'Don't be putting this in your bloody paper or you'll be sorry.'

'Well, I'll be off. Incidentally what was the score?'

'Piss off,' said Whelan with feeling.

8

Promptly at 8.30 am King rang Harris on the desk to report his successes, and give them some idea of what to expect in the morning.

'Village darts league bust up, an Indian Prince who sells Victoriana. Now all we want is crime and sex,' grinned King.

'Sounds good. Keep it up Joe,' said Harris. 'File at the same time tomorrow.'

At noon King found Mahatma 'next door'. Business was bad, he said. They'd have a couple of drinks and go and see the shop.

A couple of drinks to Mahatma, who didn't appear to have any Muslim traits, was three large ones.

Then he took King into his 'emporium' next door. It was a veritable Aladdin's cave.

'See many things here. Many junks. In jumble sale and car boots they sell this. At antique markets they sell for many pounds. So I buy at jumble sales and sell at many less pounds than antique man in main street.' Mahatma flashed his gold teeth in a big grin.

'In London and Birmingham many of relations are dealing in large items. But they have them in shop for long times. I buy and sell. I like the local people. I think they like me.

'They think me daft and call me Mr Coat. But there are many, how you say whose marbles are not collectable. In fact some are rolling off the edge of the table.

'Every day there is a man called Salt. He comes past. He is in search of marbles. He run past my emporium shouting: "It is bugger when you can't shit!" How you make of that? But I sell him old dressing gown in case it ever happen. And people come in here with polished boots and new anorak. They are pretend people. Never been up a mountain. I sell them old postcards to send to mother. It make them look like ones who know where is what. I smile at them and charge them too much. Some, they are gushing to pay. Men with silly purses which they open and diggle doggle all the coins out to the other end before reaching for their wallets. Old dolls too, very pricey. I can get middle-aged dolls and put them in a solution that make them look old.'

King looked at the Indian. 'Look, mate,' he said. 'I'm going to do a piece on this. How about Indian Prince rips off tourists?'

Mahatma gave him a golden smile. 'Just don't mention the dolls,' he said. 'The rest is fair gamings. They know. I know. We are both happy. I know my father would be happy with me.'

So will my bloody news editor, thought King. El rip-off, or whatever they say in Calcutta.

They went back next door for a drop of lunch. Mahatma looked as if he expected remuneration for his revelations. So King got them in. Doubles again. Thank Christ for exes, he thought.

The chat in the bar was as ever. 'Still out?'

'Yeah, nowt about. Seven months now. But I start tomorrow in Kendal – three days a week.'

'How do you get there?'

'No problem – get a taxi. It's only six miles.' They say there's no money about!

King was beginning to feel like a bit of female company. Notebook full, he phoned back to Keswick and the friendly Molly. She answered the bell at the Bale and chuckled: 'Where the hell are you now, Joe?'

'Just Ambleside,' he laughed. 'I'm not heading east until the morning. Can you get the night off?'

'It is my night off.'

'I'll pop round about 6pm,' said King, already beginning to feel guilty.

King replaced the phone, Mahatma left and he was chatting to the blokes in the bar. 'Rum bugger that Mahatma Coat. But you've got to hand it to him, he's smarter than the average bear,' said one.

His mate went on: 'There's always been funny buggers in the Lakes. It used to be just beards and unnecessary walking sticks. Now they're turning up with pony tails and earrings. Bunch of poofters, if you ask me.'

'Aye,' said King wisely. 'Do you know why they used to wear earrings – the old sailors?'

Blank eyes answered his question.

'It was because if they were shipwrecked on foreign shores, there'd be enough gold to give them a proper burial.'

'Well, I'll be buggered,' said the man with a shiny nose. 'Tha' learns summat every day. Nowadays they're for posers. Half the blokes walking round this town look like Errol Flynn in the Sea Hawk.'

There was the usual banter and laughter and King left for his camper. Should he really go back to Keswick and see Molly? Bollocks, he thought, a man's word is his bond.

So he headed back north, parked up and out of sheer nervousness, bought two more sticks of rock. If I carry on like this, he thought, I'll have more rock than the bloody Blackpool Pleasure Beach.

He had a brew and a shower, squirted some stinky stuff under his armpits and wandered, somewhat less than casually, round to Molly's cottage.

'Come in love,' she said. She was dressed in a skirt and jacket and he noticed she had had her hair done.

'Nicely turned out,' he grinned at her. 'We going for a meal – or what?'

'Or what, I think I'll do for a while,' grinned Molly.

'Do what?'

'Wait for something to eat.'

King was getting edgy. 'Look,' he said. 'Let's go down to the hotel and have something to eat and a chat. I'll tell you all my secrets.'

'I'm not going to tell you mine,' said Molly, with a broad and friendly grin. 'But I could do something to a nice Dover sole.'

Bloody hell, thought King. Do expenses run to Dover sole?

'You wouldn't settle for a Fleetwood dab, would you?' he joked.

They had a candlelit table at the Castleyard Hotel. The head waiter was tip-poaching, smirking through a set of uneven teeth. For once in his life King found himself tongue tied. He'd played rugby, football, cricket, got involved in public bar melees. But now, confronted with a barmaid over a candle, he didn't know what to say.

'Funny one-way system here,' he ventured. 'It makes parking a game like roller ball.'

'You're worried, aren't you love?' said Molly. 'You don't have to be. I'll look after you.'

'That's what I'm worried about,' said King, looking into his glass of Beaujolais. 'It's all too easy. I know we could go back and spend the night together. So do you.'

Molly smiled.

'But I have to go home. I have a wife and a couple of ankle snappers. I couldn't let them down.' He felt Molly's foot rubbing his shin. She had taken her shoe off.

He felt himself being aroused. In bar room terms, he had a bonk on.

Molly knew. 'I'll settle for a good night kiss – and another bottle of wine,' she laughed. 'I'm not the sort of lass to get a lad into trouble.'

King felt a right pillock. He thought – if Jock and the lads could see me bottling this one I'd never live it down.

'Tell you what kid,' he said. 'We'll finish this and go on a crawl round the locals. You'll know them all.'

'You're OK Joe,' said Molly. 'I understand. If you change your mind so be it. Pick up the bill you soft bastard.' At that moment, King didn't feel soft all over!

In the Snurter's Arms he felt far more at ease. The fire was glowing, there were no other customers. It was as peaceful as village cricket. He bought the drinks and the landlord, palefaced for a Lakeland man, looking him in the eye and said sombrely: 'Out enjoying yourselves?'

'Aye,' said King.

'You have to follow life's carnival – but march to your own drummer,' said the publican, mysteriously.

King took the drinks back to the table and said to Molly: 'What's the matter with him then?'

'You just don't bring me to the right places,' she said. 'He's miserable, Mick. The only landlord in town who always thinks his glass is half empty rather than half full. I wouldn't buy any long playing records if I were him. He looks as if he's two clean shirts away from the satin box. A grand night this has turned out to be!'

They both laughed. King more out of relief that the sexual ice seemed to have broken.

Molly asked the gaunt-faced landlord: 'Has Johnny been in, Harry?'

'Any minute, why?'

'My friend might like to have a chat with him,' said the cheerful Molly.

King looked at her. 'What are you up to?' he asked.

The girl laughed: 'Well, we found you Mahatma Coat. This one could be as good – even better.'

'How come?' asked King.

'Because he's 70.'

'So's my dad,' said King. 'Is that a big deal?'

'Is your dad flying aeroplanes upside down over the moors?'

'Well, I suppose not right at this moment,' laughed King. 'What're you trying to tell me?'

'There's an old airfield up on the tops over there,' said Molly, pointing vaguely at the wall containing the rugby fixtures and a crude plate showing the Manneken Piss, the statue of a little boy piddling into a fountain.

'OK, who is this flying ace?' said King.

'He's Johnny Bell. Made a lot of money out of whisky after the war. Hails from Scotland, but I don't know if he's one of the distilling family. They call him Ding Dong,' she said.

'They would,' said King, scenting his next piece. 'Does he always come in here of an evening?'

'And here he is,' said Molly. 'What ho Johnny! Good day?'

'Spiffing, my dear. Are you getting your oats?'

Bell was surprisingly young looking for his years. The face was lined. It had seen active service on more fronts than one. 'Who's your chum?'

Molly gave her ready smile and introduced King to the old boy.

'Pieces for the Evening Press, eh?' he said. 'Want a real goody?'

King said: 'Understand you do a bit of flying still. Not exactly Lincolnshire round here.'

'No, but more fun,' grinned the small, craggy faced man. 'Came into a spot of cash and got my own kite. Go up about twice a week these days. Keeps the old mind active. What sort of journalist are you, anyway?'

There was no hedging allowed here. 'I'm an out of work brewery rep doing a set of pieces on pubs in the north for a week or two. Then I suppose it'll be the dole until I can find something,' admitted King.

The red nose twitched and the faded blue eyes brought laughter lines around his eyes. 'Fancy a flying lesson?' he asked.

King went quiet. 'You what?' he ventured. 'You mean me go up there with you?'

'Good, you accept. Report at the drome at 10-30 am tomorrow and we'll have a look at the old wind sock,' said Bell. 'Bung-ho, must go,' he said, finishing his pint of Guinness in one and heading for the door. He threw a card on King's table and said: 'Ring me if you chicken out.'

'That does it,' King said to Molly. 'Thanks love. This could be the best one yet. I'm going.'

'Then God help you,' said his friend. 'He'll throw you all over the sky and then make you buy the beer. But if you survive it should make a cracking story.'

Survive, shit, thought King. This is the big one. He saw Molly back to her cottage, said sorry for not coming up with the expected goods, and went back to the camper to knock his stuff together for the morning . . . and dream about Biggles.

The road east was a long one. There was still snow, a lot of it, on the tops. Chicken out! King had just filled in Harris after filing his stuff. The reaction was great. 'Seventy year old battle of Britain pilot still flying sorties over the Lakes. Christ, how do you find 'em Joe? Go for it man. Remember you're not insured with us. Freelances are freelances! But this could be a winner. I'll get a snapper up there when I can. Golden weddings, you know. Old bastards fill our pages and sell our paper. Trouble is, it costs us a bottle of sparkly every time we turn up, because we've got to have them clinking glasses, with their wedding pictures on the sideboard behind them. Then and now.'

'Might be the same today,' said King. 'If David Bailey turns up to do some pix he'll want the old bastard now – climbing into his Spitfire in 1940.'

'Aye lad, but that's a bit different,' said Harris. 'Get on with it. Sooner you than me. Looping the loop over Shap and throwing up over your trousers doesn't qualify for exes.'

'Not even dry cleaning?' laughed King.

'Piss off Biggles,' said Harris. 'I'm a busy man.'

The address on the back of Bell's card was not accompanied by a map. King had some trouble finding the old airfield. It's not airfield country up there. But Bell had discovered this old emergency runway and hangar which he rented. King turned up the rocky lane and eventually came upon the old corrugated-iron shed which housed Bell's aircraft. There were weeds growing through the cracks between the concrete runway slaps.

In front of the hangar stood a light aircraft. In front of the light aircraft stood Johnny Bell. 'Pre flight checks, old boy,' he said. 'You never lose old habits. Especially when your life's at stake. Welcome.'

King could easily have turned round and gone the other way. 'What do I have to do?' he asked feebly after shaking hands with the old ace.

'Just as I bloody well tell you old boy,' said Bell. 'Check the chalk marks on the tyres for a start.'

'Chalk marks?' asked King, looking daft.

'That's right old son. We mark 'em to show they haven't shifted on the wheel in the last landing. And we check the juice to make sure there's been no condensation. That's in this little jigger,' he said. 'This is a fuel strainer. Moisture from the air will collect at the bottom of the tank. Water is thicker than fuel and could block the carburettor. That could be pretty bloody tricky. That's why we have this little plastic jar just to check.

'Now check the condition of the prop, rudder, flaps, ailerons. Can't be too careful, you know. Everything seems ticketty boo. We have an electric starter, so you don't have to go out and swing the old prop.'

'Thank Christ for that,' said King, his nerves beginning to show.

'Right,' said Bell. 'Let's get up there. See, I'll fasten you in.'

Bell climbed into the cramped little cockpit and Bell helped him with his safety harness. The old boy turned and looked like a car key, and intoned: 'Right mag, left mag, both mags.' The propeller started to turn. He released the parking brakes and opened the throttle for taxi-ing.

As there was no control tower, Bell was left to his own devices. He checked the windspeed and direction and headed for the end of his little runway.

'Oh shit,' said King – aloud.

'You what, old boy?' said Bell, stopping at the end of the take-off. 'Now listen to me. When we get up there you'll be wanting to go. It's a bit noisy, so I'll talk to you on the head set. Keep your bloody hands off everything until I say otherwise. Then I'll say: 'You have control.' You will answer: "I have control". We'll take it from there. Like riding a bike, old thing.'

Bell revved up the engine, let off the brake and powered down the runway. King closed his eyes. When he opened them seconds later the snow-covered fells were hundreds of feet below him.

'Bung-ho,' bellowed Bell. 'Here we jolly well go.'

The north westerly wind was buffeting the little Cessna about and King looked at the flying ace and said through the headset: 'Oh fuck.'

Bell laughed. 'Keep your legs together and look for those fokkers coming out of the sun,' he laughed. 'There's always wind up here. Let's give it some . . .

'Right rudder pedal down to go right. Left for left. It's just like a motor car. Not quite so fast as the old spit, though,' he said. 'I'd like a Rolls Royce Merlin under this bonnet. But this is a Cessna 152. The old Merlin would rip it apart.'

'It'd bloody rip me apart too,' said King, who hadn't yet summoned the confidence he needed.

'When I was a damned sight younger than you I'd shot down four Messerchmits over the Channel,' laughed the buccaneering Bell. 'There's a little thing in all of us that says: "Go for it, old sod".'

An updraught from a fellside hit them at around 2000 feet and King said more rude words, hanging onto the column in front of him.

'You have control,' said Bell, suddenly and with a tinge of authority.

King took the column, covered the rudders with his feet and answered: 'I have control. And I feel like Douglas bloody Bader.'

Bell laughed. 'Turn north,' he said. 'You know which that is, I presume.'

King was one of those people who always knew where north was. He didn't know why. He dipped the right wing and took control. 'Keep your bloody nose on the horizon,' said Bell. 'Forget the bloody wind. There's got to be wind. In five minutes you'll see a tarn. Turn right again then.'

King's light breakfast had settled, and he was beginning to enjoy himself. The scenery was stunning. He could see the lakes over to the west, with the Irish Sea beyond.

He made the right turn too tightly and Bell said sharply: 'Settle, Biggles. Let's get home and have a pint.'

Bell pointed out the airspeed indicator. Indicating the throttle, he said: 'Pull her back to 70 knots. I'll deal with the flaps. Give me control.'

King was quite relieved. 'You have control,' he said, trying to show worldly authority. The aircraft's altitude dropped and the ground came closer. The runway, which had looked like a tennis court from two miles loomed, and Bell dropped them in for a perfect landing. 'Right,' he said. 'Post flight checks. Got to do it right old boy.'

As the pair climbed out of the small craft a photographer was waiting for them. They posed in front of the prop, shaking hands. It wasn't the only part of King that was shaking.

'Bloody wonderful, thanks,' he said to Bell. 'Never known anything like it.'

'Beats bloody football hooligans,' said the old Wingco. 'If there was more fun and adventure in life there wouldn't be all these chappies with funny haircuts, tattooed necks and earrings. Stick to flying and rugger, old boy. Right, you can buy me a pint of wallop on your expenses.'

'You're on,' said King, his knees still shaking mildly. 'Where are we going?'

'Just one mile,' said Bell, securing the plane to a concrete stanchion, into the wind. 'I'm as ready as you are,' he laughed.

9

Bell led King to a pub that seemed the back of beyond. The moorland around was still half frozen, the snow still on the ground and the sheep sheltering their lambs. Christmas card stuff.

The bar was full of wonderful junk. 'That stag must have hit that wall at some bloody speedy,' nodding in the direction of the beast's head on a plaque.

'Don't you know any new ones?' asked Bell, nosing his double whisky and getting stuck into it. 'Enjoy it up there?'

'One of the best things I've ever done in my life,' said King. 'What do I owe you. Must have cost a fortune in juice.'

'Nothing lad. Write a good piece. Send me a copy and a picture for my wall. And come to see my again. We'll have another sortie.'

'Jeez,' said King. 'We'll be looping the loop next.'

'No, but perhaps a victory roll,' grinned the old aviator. 'I enjoyed it too. Another couple of goes and you'll be getting the hang of it. You can buy me the other half and we'll call it quits. And get down into the village tonight. It's talent night. Lovely pub this, mentioned in Wainwright's book . . .'

King took his van back onto the main road, pulled into a lay-by and wrote his air tale. He had a brew and went down into the village. He phoned Maggie and she told him: 'They're still looking for your car. How're you getting on?'

King told her. 'Bloody hell Joe, we've got kids, you know! Flying about the mountains with an old aged pensioner. God!'

'Read the piece,' laughed King. 'I'm going to talent night at the Lion tonight. Might do a bit!'

'The sooner you're back here the better,' said Maggie. 'God knows what you're up to now.'

'Watch this space,' said King, as his change ran out.

Had he been in Chelsea, King would have probably called his feeling 'Spaced out'. Up in the fells they called the pub a 'A reet 'un'. It was kind of snuggly. Not twee not trendy. It didn't smell of chips or vinegar, but you could get home-cured ham. It was in the V of the valley. Some would call it a hamlet – others 'a few houses and a pub'.

Estate agents would call it a delightful northern fell village with all modern conveniences. The Lion was of that pristine northern white. Rain-lashed-clean, frost-split whitewash. A car park at both sides. Both of modest proportions. the front door was central. There didn't seem to be any other – unless you were driving the dray.

King took his mobile home into the car park and entered. There was a good smell and a few blokes around the bar. He looked at his watch. 'Still open?' he asked.

'Like the windmill, we never shut,' grinned the chap behind the bar, whom King took to be the landlord. 'What can we get you? Large Barcardi and coke? Maybe a large malt?'

'I'll try your lager. Just a half,' said King. 'Isn't it party night tonight?'

'How do you know that?' asked the landlord. 'You on holiday or what? You certainly can't be a bloody talent scout!'

'Just travelling,' said King.

'What, a bleedin' gypsy? A New age Traveller or something?' asked the boss.

'Nowt like that,' laughed King. 'I'm having a few days off. Away from the trouble and strife and the ankle-biters. I've got a camper. Can I leave it here the night? I'm Joe, and you're . . .?'

The landlord looked him over. 'Well, you look clean. You don't look a bad old shit. I'm Alan. Stick it right in the top corner. We get busy tonight.'

'Thanks pal,' said King.

'And how do you know about our talent night anyway? It's

not in the bloody Radio Times. It's not advertised. But I'll tell you something, if you're staying you'll have a laugh. The daft buggers come down from the hills to make themselves look retarded in our clubroom.

'And other daft buggers come down from the hills to watch them do it. It's like Central Pier some weeks. You've no idea the acts that throw themselves on the boards can come up with. Eh, and get close to the fence with your caravan for Christ's sake.'

King had the feeling there was something good afoot. 'I can't sing a note, juggle or do back flips,' he said. 'But I can sit quiet-like and I like a jar or two.'

'Then watch out for the fun. It doesn't take long to hit the fan. What've you been doing?'

'Oh, flying around with a World War Two fighter ace and that sort of thing.'

'Jesus Christ, you've not been up with Johnny Bell?' said Alan, looking at King as if he had the lights on, but there was nobody in. 'You must be barmy. He should have been grounded years ago, but he keeps his hours up and there's nothing they can do. He sometimes buzzes us. Old couples sitting in the garden with their halves and ham sandwiches dive for cover. Children shit themselves and dogs take off over the fells never to be seen again. How did you get involved with that silly bugger?'

King chuckled as he looked round the cosy bar, the fire glowing, the old heavy tables polished with years of dominoes shuffling.

'Well, I'm an out of work brewery rep from down in Lancashire. I got a bit of redundancy. I've got a lovely, understanding wife who told me to bugger off for a couple of weeks and blow the cobwebs away. Do my own thing. I'm writing a few pieces for the Evening Press. I was introduced to Johnny Bell. He asked me if I wanted a waft across the sky. It was too good to miss. I think I've got a decent piece out of it. How did he really get that Cessna?'

'There were four of them came out of the RAF at the same

time,' said Alan, a tall, lean man with huge forearms. He was the sort of bloke you always agreed with.

He laughed: 'They all had some money and some flying experience. Two were flight engineers and both have since died. Johnny's mate was a pilot like he was. But he's a bit past it and just helps with the upkeep in case he wants to be nipped somewhere.

'So old Johnny has about the main use of it. Loves blokes like you he does, Likes to scare the shit out of folks.'

'Quite enjoyed it myself,' said King. 'And I'm not being smart-arsed. Tell me, what's the big deal here tonight – really? And I repeat, I can't do acrobatics, conjuring tricks or sing My Way!'

'You'll see,' said Alan. 'We get every sort of act you can imagine in there,' he indicated the clubroom with his thumb. 'We even get women producing canaries out of their drawers!'

'I can't do that either,' said King. 'I think I'll just come in as a member of the audience. I don't fancy myself as an impresario. What time's the kick off?'

Alan told him: 'Get your seat by eight or it's standing room only.'

'I'll just go and clean up and rewrite Biggles Flies North, and I'll see you later.'

He did just that. There was a dearth of rock shops and no post card stalls, so King had no cause to be side-tracked from his task.

When he returned to the pub he rang Maggie and reported all was safe. 'I've knocked out my flying experiences,' he said. 'Sounds like the Dambusters!

'Kids OK? Shithouse found the office car yet? No? Good. Keep the bastards guessing.'

'You been drinking, Joe,' asked Maggie. 'You sound on a high.'

'So would you if you'd been up with Johnny Bell. No, I'm fine. Going to a talent concert tonight.'

'Oh my God. What are you going as? Thank God I'm not

with you. If you try singing with the band you'll empty the place.'

'Roger and out,' laughed King, putting down the handset. He then had an idea. He gave Jock a ring. 'Doing anything mate?' he asked.

'Just getting pissed off and occasionally pissed,' said his buddy.

'Want a couple of days fun?' asked King. 'Can you work a 48 hour pass and get your arse up here. I'm having the time of my life.'

'So it seems. I've seen the paper,' said Jock. 'Course I can get away. They only call our house Colditz because it SEEMS to be hard to get out. In fact the camp commandant's looking at me now. What's that love? Oh, she says, go off and see your mate. Where shall I see you?'

'Leave first thing. You'll be here by mid-morning,' said King. 'I'm on the car park of the Lion. But be careful, there's a laugh round every corner.'

'I'll be there. Just one thing – what's the bloody place called?'

King laughed and told him. 'Just get up here buddy,' he said. 'We'll have a couple of days fun. And there's two bunks in the camper. Bring a bottle – and the rest's on my exes.'

'Smart-arse,' laughed Jock. 'See you in the morning, big man. Oh yes, that twassock from transport is till hunting for your car.'

'Tell him nowt,' said King. 'I might need that bugger for a day or two when I get back. Just off to the talent show. Sitheee!'

By half past seven the public bar was packed. There were seats and tables, but no elbow room at the sharp end. King walked through to the lounge which was quieter, and ordered a pint. He took the top off it and the chap next to him at the bar, wearing a nose honed from winters on the fells and a tweed jacket, said: 'On holiday, or here for the fun?'

'Well, kind of both,' said King. 'I understand there's a bit of a do in the back tonight. And I'm staying in a camper.'

'Very wise. My name's Barney. I've taken early retirement

74

after farming all my life. If you want a seat, go through now. I'll come with you.'

The pair wandered through into the clubroom and got the last corner table. 'Try never to miss this bugger,' said Barney. 'It's amazing what people think they can do. Good job Bernard Delfont's not around.'

There seemed to be huge amusement, laughter and anticipation all around. The air was far more electric than at the Karaoke night.

Everyone was chatting, smoking and drinking. King soaked up the atmosphere. A couple joined him at his table. 'How ya goin?' asked the portly gentleman wearing a sweater with a Manchester United motif on the left breast.

'Right as owt,' said King. 'Decent sort of pub, this.'

'You wait,' he said. And asked his girl what she would like to drink.

'Ooh Ducky,' she cooed. 'Absynthe makes the heart grow fonder.'

'Bollocks,' said the husband. 'You're not in full control.'

'Give me two hours and we'll see who's in control and who isn't,' she said.

This, thought King, was going to be good. He realised it was going to be even better when the first act was introduced.

A lady of generous proportions minced on to the stage and once the applause had subsided, she beamed at the audience and put her hands together. The pianist gave a small overture and King thought – God, she's an opera singer.

With no ado, the well-blessed lady, dressed in a finely flowered dress and high heels burst into full voice.

King was expecting 'Her tiny hand is Frozen'.

The rest of the audience awaited with bated breath.

And suddenly the huge woman made a noise like a cow in labour.

King looked at his chum and started to chuckle. Then the woman started snorting. She said: 'That's the British saddleback,' she said. And the audience roared its approval.

Then the lady put her hands together again like a practised

diva and gave forth. Not to some gem from La Scala. But making noises like a shire horse in pain. King looked around him and everyone was starting to giggle.

The artiste then started honking like an Aylesbury duck, and King burst out.

'Oh shit. Oh, bloody shit,' he uttered. That set the others off and in seconds everyone was heaving with laughter. The lady artiste looked quite pleased and soon started to make goat noises. 'That's the Anglo-Nubian,' she announced. King had to leave for the gentleman's water closet. It was many minutes before he could return.

By then the animal impersonator had been replaced by a tap dancer. He did a bit of a Fred Astaire on the stage and then called for a table. It was pretty obvious he had been at the pop. He appeared to be disobeying his legs.

He managed to keep on his feet, but only just on the table. 'By gum, he fills his trousers well,' said a large blonde on the next table to King. 'I reckon he's a real neck snapper.'

'Well,' said her pal, 'I wouldn't snap mine if I passed him in the corridor.'

'You're not likely to,' said her friend. 'He's fallen off the bloody table.'

After the ambulance had been called, they brought on the comedian. Unfortunately it was a bit sooner than he'd expected, having come down from the hills where he'd been doing a bit of lambing.

But he was up to the job.

'It's their own fault,' he said. 'If you buy a one-legged canary do you want a singist or a tap-dancer?

'Just got back from Blackpool. Bloody hell – so many folk on the sands tide couldn't get in. Boom, boom, that's a good 'un isn't it?

'Don't know how that song and dance man fell off't table. He's normally so careful he has a rear view mirror on his walking stick. Did you like that one?'

King couldn't believe it. A big rough farmer coming down off the fells and doing a Jimmy Tarbuck. The place was in tucks.

'Go for it Albert,' a cross-eyed man with a flat nose shouted. Albert did.

'Your missus is looking good tonight, Kev,' shouted Albert into the microphone. 'But I suppose there's many a new piston under an old bonnet!

'I've got a new address. I've re-named Lilac Cottage because it's bloody hard to get out for a drink! That's another good 'un, isn't it,' bellowed Albert.

'Mind you're lucky I'm here tonight. I've been to the doctor's. I told him I had a terrible memory. He said: "Have you?" I said "Have I what"?'

King had his pencil going. Who could believe all this could go on up in the lonely fells?

'I asked the doctor if he'd got anything for a cold and he asked my why I wanted a cold? Bloody hell, that's another good 'un.

'I told him for all the good the suppositories he had given me did, I might as well have shoved them up my arse! Christ, aren't these funny?'

They may have been corny, but the audience was loving it. So was the landlord. The till sounded like a Jewish piano. Albert chortled his way to the end of his act to a standing ovation. The last act of the night was a singer who could juggle. He had a fat belly and kept dropping his blazing torch. His 'I left my heart in San Francisco', was not exactly Tony Bennett. But passable. Bernard, a local fireman stood by the phone for the rest of the act. For King, it was a memorable night. He had another pint and headed back to his camper to write up his latest piece about life in the northern hills. His last thought as he went to sleep was: 'They'll never bloody believe this either.'

He filed a piece the following morning, raising mirth from the copy-takers. He could hear big Mabel, even though she had her hand over the mouthpiece, saying to her mates: 'Jeez, don't shove this up the tube till you've read it. I don't know where this bloke gets them. And he's not even on the staff!'

10

The morning was miserably grey – like King felt. He had a mouth like an Arab's gusset and went for a sharp walk round the village after beans on toast, tea and a good swill.

In the car park there was a tourist information map with a large red arrow pointing out: 'You are here.'

He heard footsteps behind him and stepped to one side. 'How the hell do they know we're here Pete?' said this Geordie accent.

King thought, hell here we go again. Just wait until Jock arrives.

The local tea-shop had a splendid array of postcards and Kendal mint cake in the window. The postcards were tinted sepia by long service, but they had a fresh supply inside.

King decided to have another cup of tea and sat at a small table. Two ladies in hats, the sort worn in cinema cafes in the Fifties, were in full flow.

The one with the large nose, the valour hat and a wall-eye said loudly to her friend: 'And of course she had a good address. How can anyone live without a seaview? And Henry came to a very acceptable end – his horse fell on him!'

'My Cyril likes Sunderland,' said her friend mysteriously. 'I'm not sure why. I don't think he's quite together.'

'Probably from a poor background,' said big nose. 'Lack of calcium, you know. They used to get ricketts.'

King couldn't help himself. 'I thought that was the blue stuff my ma put in the dolly tub.'

Big nose gave King a malevolent stare and said to her friend. 'I thought we were having a private conversation. It's like the

M.I.5 in here. We're being overheard. Let us away!'

Again King's book and pen were out. Both stout ladies glared at him as he left. He smiled at them and said: 'What now ladies? Going bungee jumping? Best of luck with the hang gliding!'

The small man behind the counter, almost hidden by the glass case of scones, was convulsed. 'Thanks mate,' he said. 'Not that I don't want the custom, but those two have been a right pain in the arse all week. What you doing here?'

'Bit of this and that,' said King. 'Having a break. Waiting for a mate. Doing a bit of writing. Normal sort of shit . . .'

'My name's Sid. It would be, owning a caff, wouldn't it? There's no end of bollocks goes on round here. When's your mate coming?'

'About midday,' said King. 'What's the crack?'

'You know the Lion?'

'Sort of,' laughed King. 'What's happening there next?'

'Get in there at lunchtime and you'll meet Cider Bill.'

'Not a bloody juggler?' laughed King.

'No, a complete nutter. He's booked his grave.'

'Why? Is he ill?'

'No, he just loves that churchyard. He drinks cider and Carlsberg Special mixed – in a flagon – in the bloody churchyard. He'll give you something to write about.'

After his breather he was waiting for his chum in the public bar of the Lion. The cleaners had been to work early. There was no sign of the revelries either in the bar, the lounge or the club room. The miracles of squirt-on polish and stale fag smoke removed, thought King.

He couldn't decide whether to have a heart-starter or sail straight into the lager. He decided on a heart-starter, and ordered a port and brandy. He was getting blood back into his veins, staring at the beautiful winter fells when Jock's car crunched into the car park.

'That didn't take you long,' said King.

'Joe, you can sense when a mate needs help . . .'

'And I can sense when a mate needed a change of air,'

laughed King. 'The two shook hands.

'Look, we're not staying here long,' said King. 'Got to follow the trail – "suivez la piste," as they say in France.'

'Aye man, but they don't say it in Lancashire. And you look as if you've been on a few pistes to me!'

'The name of the game, old buddy,' grinned King. 'We'll have a sandwich here and head east.'

'What's east?' asked Jock.

'Well, a few hills, a few villages, the Wainwright trail and then the sea.'

'How long? What're we going in?' asked Jock. 'And what about my car? I've not given mine back yet, you know?'

'We go in the camper. Bags of room and I'm sure you've got clean habits. The weekend's coming up, and I've heard of a pub that has a barmpots club on Saturday mornings. Anything goes. The locals are joined by the stars. They have catapult contests, airgun competitions, they play marbles in the bar, and learn juggling. And they each have to bring an item of interest to see if the others can guess it. I believe the membership includes an ice-cream merchant, an ex-M.I.5 spy, a top engineer, and a hack from a local paper.'

'Then you should feel at home,' laughed Jock. 'Where is this academy of learning?'

'It's between here and Richmond. Just relax pal, it's gone well so far.'

'You can say that again. You're a star back home. They're even laughing in the Roebuck.'

'Don't even mention that name,' said King. 'I've been having fun ever since I picked that cheque up from Cunliffe's. It just shows, old mate, there's more to life . . .'

He told his pal about the previous night's proceedings. 'It was like the London bleedin' Palladium,' said King. 'Worth a column on its own.'

Landlord Alan came in, sleeves rolled up over his large forearms and washed his hands after rolling in the barrel. Or six barrels to be precise. King introduced him to his pal.

'I think we looked after him,' said the big Yorkshire man.

'Think he was quite surprised. Always get more fun in a village than a city, you know. He said you were joining him for a couple of days. Look after him. Got to leave you. Cash and carry, you know.'

The two pals had another half, Jock put his hold-all in the van and they set off – east.

It was still cold, but the friends were well-nourished and had the heater on full blast.

King's next port of call was the Bubble and Squeak, known for some obscure reason in the village as the Rhubarb and Custard. It was in a beautiful spot, oaks and elms round the white-posted and chain-fenced village green. On the tops the wind had been as raw as a preacher's knees. Down the east side it seemed to miss them. The sun was fighting a one-all draw with the white clouds.

'Quiet for a spring Saturday,' commented Jock. 'They've all probably left early to watch Scarborough play Scunthorpe.' There were just five cars on the car park of the pretty-as-a-postcard pub. Ball games were forbidden on the village green.

'That lets you out then, Superstud,' laughed Jock.

King was glad to have his chum back for company. 'I guess this is it,' he said. 'I think this is where they have the barmpots Saturday morning club.'

'Not much here,' said Jock. 'Looks like Hamilton Academicals' car park on a good day.'

'Let's check it out,' said King. The two went into the lounge bar to be greeted by a strange scene. A portly gentleman wearing a white pith helmet was beating a spinning top around the wooden surrounds to the fading Wilton Carpet. He was being egged on by a friend wearing an old leather flying helmet and goggles.

King's sense of humour made him play it straight. Pretending he'd seen nothing amiss he asked a well-turned out lady, whom he presumed to be the boss: 'Two pints of lager, please, miss.'

She smiled at him. 'A pleasure sir, anything else? Will you be eating?'

King looked at Jock, who had turned puce and who was holding back the guffaws that were bound to follow.

'Thank you,' he said. 'That depends. May we put the camper in the far corner of the car park? Just want to stay the night. We'll pay the going rate.'

'Help yourself ducky,' said the landlady. 'Ample car park. Not a busy time of the year. Can you juggle or play marbles?'

That was it for Jock. He exploded into laughter. 'No,' he wheezed. 'But I can throw knives.'

'Just the sort of chappie we're looking for. My name's Annie. What else can you do?'

'Oh, a few rope tricks,' said Jock, as gravely as he would. He took a stern kick on the left shin from King. 'These chaps seem to be having fun.'

'The Saturday barmpots club,' said Annie. 'We have competitions and a league table. And members have to bring in an item of interest.'

'Really,' said King. 'Seeing we don't know the local customs, this is my item of interest for this week.' He pointed at Jock.

'You'll do,' said Annie. 'Honorary members. Go and get your truck parked up.'

'Truck, bloody truck,' said King as he was shown the door.

'You are a bit early,' said Annie. 'It's catapults next. Then the mad Spaniard comes in.'

King hardly dare ask: 'And, er, what's he do?'

'Pedro fights bulls.'

Jock looked nervously over his shoulder.

'Oh, not here. He does that back home. In here he's a fire-eater.'

'Well, I suppose he would be,' said Jock.

King asked: 'Any chance of a couple of pints? Like, er, before the bull-fighting, fire-eater arrives.'

Annie was boss. What she said went. And sometimes fast, King reckoned. He said to Jock: 'I'll bet she can have botherers through that door faster than a trapful of greyhounds.'

But Annie was charming: 'Two pints of bitter and a game

of quoits,' she laughed. Annie was tall and dark and looked as if she could fight sailors if the need arose. But she also looked expensive. Not short of gold rings.

The landlady went to attend to the chubby chap in the pith helmet. 'Beat him again,' he beamed. 'Forty eight seconds this week. Ho, ho, ho. that'll cost him a ding dong.'

The gentleman in the flying helmet took off his goggles and was about to cough up for the round when there was a whoosh, and flame shot through the door, almost scorching the curtains at the far window.

'Jesus Christ,' choked Jock.

'Meet Pedro,' said Annie, with a regal wave of her right hand. 'He's the local flame-thrower.'

'Get away,' said King. 'I'm just going to ring the news desk and get a snapper out here. Some folks will never have seen anything like this. A country pub, huh? More like Chipperfield Circus. Excuse me, Annie, do you have a high wire act?'

'Only the telephone pole outside. But we did have a Scotsman try to toss it one night. Thought he was at Braemar.'

'See, Jock, here's your big chance,' laughed King. 'But wait till I've phoned the Evening Press.'

By the time he got back to the bar Pedro was squirting flame all over the place from between his white teeth. Jock was cowering in a corner. 'The desk loves it,' said King to his chum. 'They're going to get a local man out now to do some pix and wire them back. The marvels of modern science.'

He said to Annie: 'I'm doing some pieces for an evening paper down in Lancashire. I'm a pub man myself, but I've never come across anything like this. Do you mind a few pictures being taken?'

'I'll go and comb my hair,' she grinned. 'When's David Bailey coming?'

'About an hour,' said King. 'Will you tell me how all this came about?'

Annie laughed: 'I don't know really. Sort of evolved. We get strangers in, the sort who never know whether to sit at a table or go out and push their grannies. They usually sit at the back over there,' she indicated a long, upholstered bench which was confronted by tables. 'They sit bemused. There's some right daft so and so's come and play silly beggers. They have to be daft to be signed in. We even have a chairman, Bernard Jump. In real life he's a top engineer. Worked all over the world. Even Russia. But in here he's as mad as the rest. We reckon he and another silly sod run the pub – that we have nowt to do with it. They even reckon they've had their own set of keys cut. And I'm not so sure about that either,' laughed happy Annie. Lager and geniality gets the better of them. Have you brought a catapult?'

'Well, no, but I can play the pipes,' said Jock bemused. 'Why were you asking?'

'Cos here's Ray. Plays soccer for Newcastle – no game today because England are playing in midweek – and cricket for Durham. They're going to do well in the county scene. Naturally Ray can't be here every Saturday. But he can on occasions. Got his own catty too. And uses ballbearings as ammo. There's affluence.'

King couldn't believe what he was listening to. But when the big athlete walked in he was even further wrong-footed. He recognised instantly an England striker. 'Hiya fellas,' said the sportsman.

'What ho,' said King. 'I'm Joe. This is Jock. We're travelling through. Not much good at pinging. Where does this take place anyway?' asked King.

'Out the back,' said Annie.

'Then watch my camper,' said King. 'I've only borrowed it.'

The Newcastle centre forward ordered a half and the six of them walked out to the car park. The chappie with the pith helmet had his own weapon, and a leather pouch with the string draw from which he selected a number of river-washed pebbles.

Leather helmet and goggles also had his own, a metal contraption rather than one carved from a hazel tree.

They were all introduced. Pith helmet turned out to be Arthur

Brown. 'Not one of the Newcastle Browns, I presume.' quipped King, already feeling in the mood.

'Oh dearie dear,' said Brown. 'And you're Joe, I believe.'

'That's me,' blundered King. 'The surname's King.'

'Oh dearie, dear,' repeated Brown, who couldn't believe he'd got his own back so soon. 'But I suppose it's been said before . . .'

'Come on you two,' laughed Ray. 'I need some target practice.'

'You can say that again,' said Annie, who had followed the group out. 'Fifteen goals a season's no good to anyone.'

'Balls,' laughed the footballer.

'Right,' said Annie. 'Preferably in the back of the net.'

This, thought King, is going to be fun. He borrowed the metal weapon and a sea-washed pebble, eyed up the tiger - shaped target that had been erected on the larch-lap fence, and let fly.

Now considering King had not used a catty since he was in the lower fourth, it wasn't a bad effort. But they were all startled by the result.

His missile shot past the tiger's tail and vanished over the fence. There was a crash of breaking glass and a loud bellow. 'Are you bastards grown up or not?' came the question, more in anger than hope. The centre forward and the fire eater were first to the back door of the pub and used their inherent pace to vanish.

Preceded by a pair of fat hands gripping the top of the six foot fence appeared a large red face. 'I don't know what the hell you all think you're doing, but this is a village for grown ups!'

King was left holding the evidence, the quarter inch thick rubber dangling from the weapon.

'Ah, well, slight accident,' he stumbled out. 'What broke?'

'What broke? My damned greenhouse again, that's what broke.'

'Perhaps I could pay for the damage,' offered King, and Jock legged if for the pub.

'One pane was it? What's that amount to?'

'One pane?' exploded the angry face. 'It'll be twelve quid for the two.'

'Two? How did it do two, one shot?'

'One in, one out the other side and in between it nearly bloody killed me. What's going on over there?'

'I don't really know,' said King. 'I've never been before.' He gave the florid man twelve pounds and left to join his partners in crime at the bar. As the photographer drew up, having driven from Richmond, King, Jock and the merry throng were playing poker dice on the bar. The chap in the goggles, who had not proffered his rank, name or number, was practising marbles on the carpet.

The photographer, recognising Ray immediately, said: 'Good God.' The chap with the pith helmet asked him: 'Do you want me with this on or off?' Jock could be heard hooting with laughter in the gentleman's water closet.

They posed for daft pictures – even Ray the star. The two barmpots kept their hats on, Annie looked glamorous and King was in the pictures only to add authenticity to his pieces.

The Spanish flame thrower took another mouthful of whatever spirit it is he used and gave the snapper some special effect. A couple of carloads of elderly customers called in, took in the scene in disbelief and went into the lounge for a long decision on where to sit before ordering their two shandies, three Britvic oranges and a diet Coke to go with their cheese ploughman's lunches.

Annie said: 'Look out lads, here's Floyd. See he's got his wife with him. He's in every night. Never used to take Gladys out at all. Now he takes her out twice a year! I asked him about this. Know what he said? "There's got to be give and take in marriage". I'd give him give and take. I'd give him one round the ear'ole. Mind, he's funny though. He had it round the village he'd bought her a moped and a knapsack so she could go off and seek her fortune,' said Annie.

Floyd walked in and, straight-faced, ordered: 'A pint of

bitter pet and a pot of bird seed for the parrot. She's been squawking all morning.'

It was too much for King and his chum. They left rolling with laughter for the van. Jock looked bemused. King, used to life in the fells by now, started to write up his notes for the next episode.

11

The next morning they went in for a heart-starter. Annie was there already, well spruced, rings on her fingers and a large opal in a choker at her neck.

'Who dressed you this morning?' quipped Jock.

'Don't get Clever Dickie,' said Annie. 'It's Sunday. They'll all be coming out for roast beef and Yorkshire pudding. No imagination, you know, English folk, Still, we do us own fresh vegetables. If we didn't open early they'd be queuing up. We tend to turn a blind 'un to licensing hours round here.

'In fact Dave, the village bobby, will be in for his pint at about eleven. No more tricks up your sleeve shooting up the neighbourhood, I take it?' she asked with a smile.

King shuffled his feet. 'Well, it wasn't really my fault. I just paid for the damage.'

'Aye, and you fired the bloody shot I understand,' said a voice from the door.'

Annie said: 'PC Dixon, how nice to see you're patrolling the area. Would you be partaking . . .?'

'Bitter. Pint, please,' said the big smiling chap, walking to the bar. 'Hey up lads, I'm the local sheriff. I just don't carry my badge on a Sunday. Understand you're doing a bit of writing.'

'Aye, here and there,' said King. 'I'm going round looking for silly so and so's – and there seems enough round here.'

'Got involved with the Saturday Barmpots then?'

'Could hardly miss it,' said King. 'I'm looking for a line for next week though. Anything unusual on the patch?'

'The next village is Reeth,' said Dave. 'Go to the village

and ask for Mick. Ask him about his hollybush.'

'Why?' asked King. 'You can't go up to people and ask to see their hollybush.'

'Mick will know what you're talking about. He'll make you laugh if that's what you're looking for. He's a big lad, but his dad were six foot nine and had to sleep in t'greenhouse.'

Jock looked at King. 'I think we're off again on something daft Joe.'

'That's what we're here for,' said King. 'But we'll stay here for us dinners.'

The bar filled quickly. The two chums stood in the snug, King listening to the conversations around him. At a small table near the window sat two middle-aged women, members of the twin-set brigade.

One said: 'Ooh Hilda, have you ever had your whims pampered?'

Her mate replied: 'Not lately. I think he's been dislodged by activity.'

'Christ,' said King. Jock spluttered. He'd done a lot of spluttering in the last 24 hours. He began to realise he didn't always listen to what was going on around him.

The first of the twin sets, the one with the blue rinse, carried on: 'His idea of a holiday was to write to the National Trust to see if we could have a weekend break in Chorley.'

Her friend countered: 'I think mine's going to end in the loopy farm making daisy chains. I asked him if he was coming out for lunch and he said he had some tomatoes to see to. How do you see to a tomato?'

The two pals looked at each other. King was surreptitiously making notes. 'I reckon my next piece is going to be: "Heard at the bar".

'That is, unless this hollybush means anything. Shall we stay or go?'

'Stay for a bit of that wee beefy,' said Jock. 'We can find a hollybush any time.'

PC Dave joined them again. 'Come across anything?'

'Few bits and bobs,' said King. 'Ever get any bother from

the blokes on the coast to coast walk?'

'Only once,' said Dave. 'One lot walking across met up with a mob doing the drovers' way from Scotland to Devon. This lot had about two hundred sheep with them and were led by a bloke with an accordion. All he could play was Flower of Scotland and there was a bit of a fracas. They caught up with him at Hawes on Market Day and chucked him in the river. Mind, you know what Hawes market day is like. Tuesday is no-go day for the weak-willed or foolhardy.

'Then there was the Glorious Twelfth last year. This lot were ambling across when the shooting started. They scattered quicker than the grouse and hid behind a wall. All day they were there. Didn't come out until the shooting had stopped. Don't suppose they'd ever heard of a white hanky on a stick!'

'Well, that'll do for another,' said King. 'Any other local barmpots?'

'Well, there's Honest Hecky who does a handstand with his golden retriever. But that can't be very interesting.'

'Why does he do it?' asked King.

'Probably because he's crackers,' said Dave finishing his pint and ordering another. 'I mean, it's not even a good trick. The best thing he ever did was chase their Nellie round t'caravan site for an hour before catching her. She'd forgotten to put his steak and kidney pudden in the oven for his tea.

'Mind, Hecky wasn't that bright. He thought a back-packer was a coal man.

'Then there was big Jed. His wife stopped his tap for falling out of the bedroom window twice in one afternoon.'

'You mean stopped him going out?' enquired King 'Because he was drunk?'

'No, because he were only wearing one wellington,' said Dave.

Jock had to sit down. 'You see his wife's mother was from one of these peculiar religious cults – the Methodies, or somebody.

'No, it's a funny place up here alright,' said Dave. 'I reckon this pub is a branch office of the Devil himself. But it's not half a good crack.

'Look out, here they come!'

King and Jock ducked instinctively and looked at the window. Some thirty walkers were marching on the pub, stout-booted, woolly bobble-hatted.

They all wore small, neat, sensible rucksacks. Most carried walking sticks. Many of the sticks had twee badges nailed to them. 'I've been to Austria, Alpen-guide, the Matterhorn,' that sort of thing. Most of the sticks – or their bearers, had not been much further than Great Shunner Fell or Ingleborough.

' "Lord Winston's Walking Tours," we call 'em,' said the policeman. 'I don't know why. But they're a bunch of Wallies. I can see one or two ending in the river if they come poncing around like that on club day. Mind, they always pay their bill. They have to sit outside though, because they bring their own sandwiches.'

'I don't believe all this,' choked Jock. PC Dave said: 'Hang on here, it's William Afford. We call him Bungalow Bill.'

'Why's that?' asked King, naively.

'Because he's got nowt upstairs,' laughed the jolly constable. Since he fell off his moped he's walked round the graveyard everyday checking he's not in there. Give himself such a huge hernia he could rest his arm on it. Celebrated his wedding anniversary with a sponsored bottle-wash, hoping to raise money for hernia relief. He even bought a little mop on a stick to do the job. But folks still took their empties to the bottle bank. I mean, who the hell wants their bottles washed? Good old Bungalow Bill!'

King said: 'I'm going to use some of this. You don't mind?'

'Just don't name me,' said Dave. 'We've a new Super, and he's a bit keen. He'll soon learn round here though.'

Bungalow Bill walked into the bar and nodded at the assembly.

'How's it going, Bill?' asked Dave.

'Me, you know,' said the small man, wearing a chunky blue sweater and watery eyes.

'Aye,' laughed the policeman. 'Tha's had a bad back ever since you put up that notice: "All scaffolding undertaken".

And where's your Ernie having his legs straightened?'

'Oh, he's not so bad now. I think it must have been 24-hour Parkinson's disease,' said the rheumy-eyed Bill. 'He get's a disability allowance now, and it seems to have helped a lot.'

'I'll bet it does,' said Dave. 'He'll be playing football next. I reckon the thought of weights gives him scales.'

King had already jotted the lot down. It was going to be The Laughing Policeman bit. Jock was not for moving.

A large red-faced man entered the bar, obviously a friend of Dave's.

'How's it this morning, Max?' grinned Dave. 'Took a load aboard last night, didn't you?'

'My head feels like a tiddly wink,' said the newcomer to the company. 'Just as well I didn't go out in the old jam jar.'

The two pals decided to stay the night and venture forth the following morning to find Hollybush Mick. They wondered why nobody would tell them what was behind it.

'Sounds a bit prickly to me,' said Jock.

'God, man, you're getting worse than this lot,' said King. 'I'm having an early night anyway and getting all this stuff together. I'll bet Wainwright never had this much fun.'

That evening in the snug things soon warmed up again. It was PC Dave's day off, and he was there again. 'Thought of one that'll make you chuckle,' he said. 'You'll have realised there's a smithering of nutters round here. I was talking to a bloke in the Post Office the other day about the weather forecast. He informed me there are some sixty references to wind in the Oxford dictionary, but that it would rain or go dark before morning!'

PC Dave introduced the pair to a middle-aged couple, both drinking halves of Guinness. 'This is Len and Lucy. Lived here all their lives,' he said.

Lucy asked: 'What are you two up to then?'

'Bit of a break,' said Jock.

'My God, every time this one comes back he seems unsettled. He should bloody well stay at home. The rest of the year he's a raving dullard,' she said, nodding at her husband.

Len's face never changed. 'She buys jelly babies by the pound and asks for all the black ones. She reckons she gets more jelly on the black boys,' he said, without an emotion showing. 'But there we go, why worry about money when you father's got piles?'

King, Jock and the policeman burst into laughter. King turned his back to the company and made some quick notes in his pad on the bar.

Lucy added: 'He's got a speech and language disability I reckon. He has no time-served apprenticeship skills. I think he's probably retarded, apart from a fortnight a year at Morecombe when he goes bananas and appears to have got a grasp of things. I think he's been sent to annoy me by a panel of experts.'

Len sank his Guinness, called up two more and said, straight-faced 'I can even be stupid in Latin. She's been putting it about that I'm daft for years.'

Lucy countered: 'He only looks like that because I have to iron his forehead before he comes out! Laugh, you miserable sod.'

Len's face never changed.

'I think his brain is in some sort of different zone,' cracked Lucy.

And King and Jock cracked up. 'Why weren't these two up at the talent night? They'd have won the Rose of Montreux.'

'No need,' said Dave. 'They're like it all the time. Folk see their car outside and come in to listen.'

Len's face never flickered. 'She's either got mad cow disease or anthrax,' he said. 'Been the same since I bought her a nasal hair clipper for Christmas.'

'Take no notice of him,' Lucy hit back. 'I might have a nose snipper, but I got him a signed degree in breaking wind. He's got low habits, you know. Even growls when he's hungry. And he's short for his age. He's 63 now, you know. Ooh, he disturbs me. He went to have the cat welded the other day!'

'The cat welded?' choked King. 'What the hell do you mean?'

'I think he meant gelded. Thought it was a bloody horse.'

The chuckling chums returned to the van for the night. King got his notes written up. They made more than the required number of words, but he said to Jock:' The hell, they'll sub it down. I'm just going to get stuff over when I get it, leave them to decide when they use it. I'll tell the desk early doors we're going to find Hollybush Mick and we'll take it from there.'

'My stomach hurts,' said Jock. 'Oh dearie dear . . .'

The couple slept like babies in the cosy camper. King was up at 7.30am to shower, make a pot of tea and check through his notes.

An hour later the pair were in the pub enjoying what they call a full northern breakfast – bacon, eggs, Cumberland sausages, black pudding and a fried slice. Suspecting what was coming they declined the porridge. King used the phone to call Harris and came back beaming.

'They're dead pleased, Jock,' he said. 'I've filed all yesterday's nonsense. I've been told if anyone needs a bob or two to open up, to offer it. I reckon that means an increase on exes. We might get a champagne supper out of it yet.'

'Champagne! The way I feel I could do with a bottle now.'

Annie vanished and came back with a bottle of bubbly. 'Open that,' she said. 'I think we all need one – and that's not on the bill.'

The bubbles gave them an early burp, clearer heads and a zest for the day to come.

King paid Annie what was left of the previous night's bar tab and for the breakfasts. He offered overnight rent for the trailer but was told to leave, in man's talk. They did, both giving her a peck on the cheek.

'We'll be back,' said King. 'I mean that. Never had so much fun. But I ain't playing catapults next time.'

The road up the valley was difficult for two dry-mouthed travellers. There was still a deal of snow on the hills but down by the byres the young lambs were finding their uncertain legs to their po-faced mothers.

'I wonder what this wee Hollybush Mick does,' said Jock. 'I hope there's a pub. I could murder a lager.'

They found Reeth village, another pretty place with an attractive wide open village green, a low war memorial, a chapel with a bit of a bell tower and a village seat that had been passed by the parish council. It was on the river Swale and sported a sturdily buttressed stone bridge over the cold-looking water that flecked and swirled under it.

They tucked the camper away on the car park and walked along the green, passing an elderly gentleman wearing a muffler and cap, an anorak and being towed by a gasping spaniel on a lead.

'Morning,' said King. 'This may sound a bit strange, but I'm looking for a bloke called Mick. Lives in a cottage near here. Gets about a bit. We were sent by some of his chums down the valley. We're doing a few articles for the evening paper.'

The old boy looked at them and grinned. 'I reckon tha's been sent to see Hollybush Mick,' he said.

'That's it,' said King. 'But it sounded such a daft thing to ask.'

'Dunna worry. Mick lives over there, two cottages back. He's in too. I've just been talking to him. He's a joiner.'

The intrepid pair sallied forth and found the cottage indicated. A big jovial-looking man in a tartan shirt and the statutory flat cap was working in his garage.

King walked into the drive and said, feeling uneasy: 'You Hollybush Mick?'

The jovial face looked up and said: 'I think that's what they call me these says. Can I help you lads?'

'I hope so,' said King. 'I'm from the Evening Press. This is my buddy Jock. We're looking for fun and laughter and tales of country folk. I understand you've one to tell – and why they call you what they do.'

'The Twichin' Witch is open,' said Mick. 'Let's go and have a livener. It's not much of a tale anyway. Who told you, that bloody policeman?'

'Something like that,' said King. 'Come on, we both need one anyway. We had a champagne breakfast, this morning, and it tends to leave you with a bit of a thirst.'

'Champagne breakfast! You must have been at Annie's. She likes to join the customers in fun and games, you know.'

It was quite a long walk, but they came across another typical northern pub with a typically northern landlady. 'Hiya Bet,' said Mick. 'Give us three pints of lager.'

King paid. These expenses were wonderful.

He introduced King and Jock to the landlady. 'These lads are doing a bit of local journalising. Looking for a good tale or two,' he beamed.

Bet said: 'then I reckon they've come to the right place.'

The trio sat at a low table at the back of the public bar, and King asked: 'How did you get this name "Hollybush"? It is a bit unusual.'

'So was that night,' laughed Mick, his face beaming with the memory."It's nowt really, but a tale gets around, and gets better with the telling. I was in here one night with Clubfoot Pete. We'd had a few. Perhaps more than that. And he goes and tells me his chimley needs sweeping.

'Well, with him having a clubfoot and me having a ladder, it all seemed so easy. Me dad had always told me you never need a chimley sweep if you know where you can nick a hollybush. Well, I knew.

'At closing, me and Clubfoot goes out onto t'edge of the common and we hack off this young hollybush. Clubfoot, who had been as good as gold till then, asked me why we needed the bush.

'I told him: "We're going to sweep your chimley. I'll bring me ladder and you find a brick. I'll see you at your cottage in 10 minutes.

'Sowe meet there, me with a ladder and a length of rope and him with a brick. So I ask him which chimley it is that needs cleaning and put up the ladder.

'We went inside and taped newspaper all over the fireplace so not so much as a spider could escape.

'Then I says to Clubfoot: "Then tie the brick to the rope and go indoors and let me know when the bush comes through". So he goes inside and goes up the ladder and drops the brick, the rope and the holly bush down the offending chimley.

'And I calls out: "Is it through yet Pete?" He comes to the cottage door and says nowt's happened. Well, I can't understand this.

'Then all of a sudden there's a great wail and a scream and this old dear runs out of her cottage next door looking like Al Jolson. Black from top to bottom with mad, staring eyes. He'd only told me the wrong chimley.

'Well, this old dear is running around and round, frightening passers-by to death, and I gets off me ladder and goes to look in her cottage. It was worse than a wash-house in a coalmine. Soot everywhere.

'It was a quarter of an inch thick on the table. What had been her supper was buried. She came running back into the front room as Clubfoot reappeared. "Has something gone wrong?" he asked.

'Old Mrs Beamish was still letting off a tremendous din. You know how you do daft things in a moment of panic? Well, Clubfoot only asks her if she was having her supper!'

Jock was wheezing. King was trying to write.

Mick carried on: 'She said: "Supper, bloody supper. If you can find my cheese sandwich under that lot you can have it."

'Clubfoot picked up a plate, blew an inch of soot off its contents and said: "Er, was this it?"

'By now, the place was in an uproar. The neighbours had heard the commotion and called the police. That's how Big Dave knows about it all.

'The old dear was still wailing, so were the police car sirens. There were blue lights flashing and a sergeant from Richmond came in and asked who has done this. I had to raise my hand.

'When it all settled, Clubfoot and me spent the whole night cleaning the old dear's front room.'

'Did she ever get her cheese and onion sandwich?' asked King, cheekily.

'Piss off,' laughed Mick. 'I hope you know these are on you.'

'OK,' said King, 'but I'm not paying for the hollybush too.'

12

They parked in the public car park, feeling they knew the local constabulary well enough, and went back to the Witch in the evening.

Bet was in full flight when Mick joined them. 'Have you told 'em about the Invisible Man?' she asked, wiping tears out of her eyes with a bar mat.

'The what?' asked King, sniffing another day's expenses and a good laugh.

'There's this twassock down at the Farmer's whatsit at Swanley Bottom. He has an invisible mate. He's brilliant. You never see him.'

'Well, you wouldn't,' said Jock.

'I'm telling you no more,' said Hollybush Mick. 'Get there by midday if you want a laugh.'

Bet asked the lads: 'Are you staying around here?'

'We've got a camper on the car park across in the village,' said King.

'Put it on ours if you want, it'll be safer,' said Bet. 'There's some nutters round here. Look at him in the front bar.'

They craned their necks and saw a smart-looking chap in a sports jacket.

'We had a pub quiz. The first question was: "What was Ghandi's first name". He bellowed "Goosey, Goosey". We lost. Looking at him you wouldn't think he preferred Dancing Queen to The Man from Laramie.

'The other night the chat at the bar turned to animals. He was asked his favourite and shouted: "Bunny Girls", and laughed at himself for about five minutes.

'A lot of inbreeding, you know. He's up and down like the Hilton lift. Dead sane sometimes. Completed barmy others. Makes life interesting. But they must be an endangered species.

'Funny Farm Fred was in the other day and the colonel was doing his Times crossword. He said: "What's that chappie's name? The clue is Egon, to do with cooking. Five letters". Tosspot there shouted: "Toast".'

'Good God, looking for dumb stories round here must be easier than signing on for the Dole. We had an Irishman here who entered the local half marathon for charity. Thirteen miles, like. He'd done 10 before he took it in there'd been a false start!'

'Here we go again,' said Jock. 'I hope you got that lot down. If this is a success, I'll settle for the TV rights.'

'If you're moving on to Swanley Bottom I'd have some of Bet's broth before you leave,' said Hollybush. 'Keep you going all day, it will. That thick she has to stir it was a navvie's shovel.'

The pair finished their drinks, took directions, ordered a bowl of broth apiece, which was certainly a spoon-stander and came with a large warm bread cob, and then took their leave.

'This is getting beyond me,' said Jock. 'I don't know how you've kept it up.'

'Well, I look on it as a break that hopefully is paying for itself. I ring Maggie and the kids each night and go into each day with wide open innocent eyes. It's what happens after that that can become a bit of a problem. But I keep in touch with the desk and file my stuff on time. That way we're all happy.'

They found The Farmers in a narrow lane, under some trees by a swiftly flowing brook. 'How will we know when we've spotted the invisible man?' asked Jock.

'He'll probably have bandages round his face, be wearing a mac and gloves, and sunglasses,' said King, flippantly. 'Just wait for it pal, that's the trick.'

The Farmers was bigger than it looked from the outside and offered a friendly lounge bar with cricket memorabilia adorning the walls. They even had an old Len Hutton blazer and a picture of Fred Trueman coming up out of the pit demanding: 'Let me get that bloody Lancashire.'

The landlord was a young fellow, pleasant-faced, open neck shirt and slacks. He made them welcome and served their drinks.

'Nice part of the country, this,' ventured King. 'Bet there's a few characters round here. We've come across from the west coast and met some amazing people. In fact, I'm thinking of doing a bit of a book there's that many of them.'

'Hang around,' said the licensee, who introduced himself as Kevin. 'Anything can happen here. They say there isn't a pub in England that hasn't got a few characters, and I reckon I've got my share. We all have round here.'

'We've met Hollybush Mick,' admitted King, wanting to look less than a daft stranger.

'That's nowt,' laughed Kevin. 'We've got some world beaters here.'

The two chums stood at the bar chatting. It was about 12.46 when the gravel crunched and an old Jaguar, in beautiful condition skidded up to the front window. It was yellow with the old crinkled bonnet.

The pair retired to a seat away from the bar and waited. Was this the invisible man?

A middle aged chap wearing a sporting cap, a clipped moustache and a yellow tie that matched the car breezed in.

'Good morning, Kevin,' he beamed.

'Morning Clarrie,' said the landlord, politely.

Clarrie announced: 'I think I'll have a gin and thinners today.' And turning to his right, he said: 'And what about you Alec.'

King and Jock looked over their shoulders. There was nobody else in the bar. They looked at each other.

'Good man,' said Clarrie. 'That's two gin and tons. Lovely morning.'

'Couldn't be better,' said Kevin, glancing at the pair who were starting to chuckle again.

'You'll both be having ice and lemon I take it?'

Clarrie glanced to his right and nodded. 'For us both,' he said.

Kevin put the two gin and tonics on the bar, iced and lemoned, and said: 'Been for a walk then?'

'Not yet,' beamed Clarrie, removing his cap and placing it on the peg in the corner. 'Alec's had trouble with Marion, haven't you old man?'

By now Jock's asthma was returning. He decided to brave it out and went back to the bar. 'Morning both,' he said.

'And to you, old boy,' said Clarrie. 'Out for a run?'

'Aye, all of us,' said Jock. King had to find the toilets.

When he returned Jock was in earnest conversation with Clarrie who was just introducing him to 'Alec.'

'He's had a rough time lately, haven't you, old boy?' Jock was left staring at a blank space as Clarrie finished his drink. It was only then he realised that both glasses had been emptied. He rejoined King at the table.

'I swear he only drank the one, but both were empty,' he said. 'He had me talking to someone who wasn't there. Either I'm going balmy or I've been on this trip with you too long.'

It was too good for King to miss: 'How do you mean Jock?' he asked his mate. 'I saw you talking to those two blokes at the bar.'

Jock looked again and burst into a howl of anguished laughter as Clarrie ordered two more gin and tonics. He thought: 'I'm going to watch this.'

'This is unreal, Joe,' he said to his pal. The next time he looked at the bar the Invisible Man's glass was empty and Clarrie was just finishing his.

'Must be off then Kevin,' he said, pulling his cap on at a rakish angle. 'We've got to sort out Alec's bit of bother. Come on old boy,' he said, putting an arm around nothing visible and walking to the door.

There is a northern phrase, not in polite use, called gob-smacked. That's what King and Jock were.

'Er, was that the Invisible Man we've just met?' asked King, a bit nervously.

'Aye, that's him,' said Kevin. 'Nice chap!'

'Bloody hell,' said Jock.

'It's quite amazing,' said Kevin. 'Clarrie always orders for the 'two' of them. Yet nobody ever sees Alec drink his. He's damned clever at it. We've had trained observers and the Invisible Man has always emptied his before Clarrie. Nowt so queer as folk!'

'Look mate,' said King. 'I'm doing a series on unusual pubs for the Evening Press. I've got to use this.'

'Sure,' said Kevin. 'You can quote me, name the pub, name Alec, but for God's sake don't identify Clarrie. We don't want any law suits. Call him Gungha Din or something.'

'We've already had a Mahatma Coat,' laughed King.

'I think I'm getting out of this game,' said young Kevin, holding his forehead. 'Are you eating?'

'Two beef sandwiches and a bowl of chips between us, but later,' said Jock. 'I don't want to start laughing on a full stomach again.'

It was now downhill to the coast. 'Where now?' said Kevin.

'Only vague plans,' said King. 'We'll get through Richmond and follow the route of his worship.'

'His Worship?' queried Kevin.

'Aye,' said King. 'We're following Wainwright's Coast to Coast Walk, and looking for dafties on the way.'

'You're in the right area,' said Kevin. 'Stop off at the next village. Have a look in the Plume of Feathers. There's a chap goes in there with a dog called Smedley.'

'So what,' said Jock. 'Lots of men with doggies around here.'

'Not like this one,' said Kevin. 'I'll go and get you your sandwiches.'

The two sat sipping their beer when two women in their forties came in. They were both dressed casually. One in jeans and one in a skirt.

They all nodded at each other. 'I'll take the skirt,' said Jock quietly.

'Toss you for it,' said King.

And from their table they listened to the two women at the

bar. 'My Jack's a great wine lover. He's said he's going to dig a wine cellar. I reckon he just wants it to bury my mother in.'

'At least that's constructive,' said her friend. 'My Neil wanted something for the shed roof, and a bloke came to the door. He said: "It's no good talking to her, she thinks wriggle it in is corrugated iron!" Well I ask you. How would you feel? Wriggly tin indeed!

'He think's I'm daft. We needed this bit of planning permission. On Saturday home he come with this bit of stuff. "She's a solicitor", he told me. I know the only sort of soliciting she does.

'Now the cheeky bugger makes light of it. He refers to her as Laura Norda. Must think I'm backward.'

'You don't suspect him of . . . do you?' asked her friend.

'Fiddling.' said the first one. 'Just because she was wearing an informative blouse! That's what attracted him. Active? He thinks radio active is switching on Jimmy Young.

'Anyway he'll be away soon. He's got an attractive job as a double glazing salesman in Belfast. That should be worth a bob or two.'

The couple ate their sandwiches and left. 'That'll do for a couple of paras,' said King. 'I wonder why this Smedley dog is so precious. Let's go find out.' They parked on the moors and went for a bracing walk. 'Do you know, in spite of all the fun we're having, I want to get home,' said King.

'You've a bit to go yet,' said Jock. 'You can't say it's been an unsuccessful mission. Look at the stories you've got out of it. The folks you've met. You'll be back, one day, to see them again.'

'Happen,' said King. He was missing Maggie and the kids. 'This is lovely up here. But I reckon on Morecombe Bay too today. I miss the sea breeze you know, Jock,' he said. 'It's OK swallocking your way over the countryside. But I like it where we live. I'm getting maudlin! Let's get on with this job. Where was that village where this bloke has a dog. Mind, I can't see a tale in that.'

'The dog can,' joked Jock. They were back to normal.

The pair drove on. The countryside was beautiful in the spring. They found the village. It didn't take them long to find the pub. Black and white it was. So was the barmaid. A lovely lass of about 18 with long dark hair.

'And what can I do for you gentlemen?' she asked as they approached the old oak bar.

'Well, I'd fancy a . . .'

'Shut it,' said King to his chum. 'We'll have two pints of lager please miss. Lovely part of the world, this.'

'Yes,' she said with a smile. 'Everywhere's lovely. You've just got to look at it in the right way. I'm going to Cyprus next week for a holiday with my boyfriend. The sun will be out. We'll go on boats and things like that. But it'll only be beautiful in its own way. If you want sun, jump on a jet and get some. But you'll always come back. Do I sound serious? Ever since I stopped smoking the world has looked different. I don't see things through a haze any more.

'There were three blokes over here last week on holiday. Supposed to be walking. I don't know how much they did, but they were in here a lot. Sat along the back there,' she said. 'I called them Freeman, Hardy and Willis.'

'Why's that?' asked King.

'Well, they were a good advertisement for showing their soles, rather than walking on them.'

'And what's your name?' asked Jock.

'I'm Jackie,' the girl smiled. 'You two on holiday?'

'Sort of half and half,' said King. 'You've got to be a bit careful with this drinking and driving. So we tend to park up. Got a camper. Anywhere we can leave it here?'

'Hang on, I'll ask the boss,' smiled the pleasant Jackie, pulling her tresses off her shoulders.

In a minute she was back. 'Arthur says you can leave it here,' she said. 'Are you about for long?'

'Probably just overnight,' said King. 'See you this evening.'

The pair went for a rest. King did his notes. Jock snored.

'Christ man, can you do that in Gaelic?' King chided him.

They were in the bar early doors, waiting for the man and

his dog. With the clock going forward, it was still light, the sun settling cosily behind the western fells.

'I'm hungry,' said King. 'Let's order something.'

Jackie gave them a menu and they both chose rump steak. They both fancied a gin and tonic and got on with it.

'Look out,' said Jackie. 'If you want a laugh, here it comes. Arthur and Smedley.'

The couple feigned disinterest as the large man walked into the bar. King glanced across and his eyes widened. Jock's gaze followed him, and he gave a great snort, trying to camouflage it with a blow into his hankie.

The man was powerful. Five foot ten of Yorkshire beef, wide shoulders and a waxed jacket. His heavy walking shoes were well polished. But it was the dog . . .

It trailed behind him on a rope. On wheels. It was a toy. The sort you'd give a three year old for Christmas. He lifted the inanimate object onto the vacant barstool at his side and said: 'There we are Smedley, your favourite stool.'

The two chums were wide eyed. They didn't know whether to laugh or leave. But having ordered their steaks they had to stay anyway.

It was King's round. With tears pouring out of his eyes he went to the bar and said to Jackie: 'Two more Gee and Tees, all in.'

He nodded to the man with the dog and said: 'Good evening.'

'Evening,' he replied. 'It's not all plain sailing, is it?'

'Well, I suppose not,' said King, by now totally confused.

'I said to my wife this afternoon: "You can get stuffed". And she said to me: "It's not everyone likes cucumber". What the hell do you make of that?'

King said: 'Tricky one, that. Nice dog you've got though.'

'Yes,' beamed the big fellow. 'Meet Smedley. Lovely little doggy, aren't you Smedders?' he said.

King and Jock looked at each other. 'Glad I'm not driving tonight,' said King. 'I don't think I'd make it to the next corner. I can't see through my tears.'

King approached the bar again, fascinated. 'Nice wheels he's got,' he offered.

'And he has his own barstool,' said Smedley's owner. 'We always sit in the same place old boy, don't we? Would you like a drink of water then?'

King, hearing Jock hooting at the table had to leave. The two were immersed in silent laughter. Jackie looked at them and had to leave the scene too.

King tried to pull himself together and approached the man and toy dog at the bar again.

'If it's not too daft a question,' he said, 'why do you bring a toy dog out?'

'My name is Simpson,' said the large man. 'Smedders is my friend. We go everywhere together. I've had him since he was a puppy. Nothing unusual in that.'

'Oh no,' said King. 'But I'm writing a few articles for a paper and thought this, er, Smedley might come under the unusual pets section.'

'Unusual?' said Simpson. 'I don't see anything unusual in Smedders, do I old chap,' he said, scratching the dummy under the throat. 'But I can't be staying for interviews. Got to be off, haven't we Smedders?' He lifted the imitation terrier off its stool, put it on its four wheels and towed it out.

The pair roared with uncontrolled laughter for a full minute. When Jackie returned, she said: 'See what I mean? There's the odd eccentric up in these hills.'

'I don't think I can eat now,' said Jock. 'I'm done. My God, you've bought me up to a rare place Joe. They'll never, ever, believe this one back home.'

'They will when they read it in the Evening Press,' grinned King. 'The trouble is I might be helping circulation. I may well be losing it for them. A lot of their customers will be coming up here nutter-hunting.'

'Aye man, but they won't weedle them out of the woodwork like you do,' said Jock.

In the end they managed their steak. Good Yorkshire beef.

Chips from real peeled potatoes, not frozen rubbish or oven baked.

They were just finishing when in walked a moon-faced couple of middle-aged plodders.

The chap wearing a sort of tartan sports jacket, his wife sporting the obligatory twin set. 'Timeliness is a courtesy to others,' I always say, said the male moon-face.

'Time!' exposulated his wife. 'You're nowt but a well organised wastrel. I'll have a sweet sherry. And that Jerry Harrison's got suspicious eyes.'

'Haven't you noticed? When he's had two pints they're suspicious.'

'Suspicious?'

'They're watching one another.'

'You daft beggar,' he said.

'Anyway, how've you got out of your duties today?'

'I said I had to make up four for bowls.'

'In March?'

'I told her it was on Astraturf and we used floodlights. And I said I'm not on my keep-fit thing. That helped. They like us fit at the yard.'

'Bloody hell,' gasped Jock. 'He's to fell running what John Inman is to rugby league.' He looked at his mate who was busily scribbling. 'He'll never be on "It's a Question of Sport",' said Jock.

The moon-faced couple at the bar were getting fractious. For no good reason the female half, well-trousered, told him severely: 'You make me sick. I think you've got colic. That's probably why you fart in your sleep.'

'You mean flatulence, like the Queen Mother has,' he said.

Owl-like she looked at him. 'How do you know that?'

'Bloke in a pub told me,' he said. 'Flatulence is a good word.'

'Oh, go and rake your grass. I've had enough of this already,' said the female half. They drank up and left.

'What do you make of that?' asked the amiable Jackie. 'They're always at it. He doesn't get away with much, but he's a different bloke when he's on his own.

'He escaped the other morning by saying he was taking his stick for a walk. He'll not pull that one again.'

13

The evening, and other things, had crept up on the intrepid pair. They were lying in the dark of the warm camper, at peace with the world, when Jock said: 'Joe, where the hell are we?'

'Between here and there,' said King. 'Go to sleep man, I'll show you a map in the morning.'

'All I reckon is that I'm going to leave here with a scorched cheque book,' moaned Jock.

'Come on man,' said King. 'I've never met a tight Scotsman yet. Always first to the bar, they are. It's costing you nowt except your grub and booze. We're living rent free, no hotel rooms, no overheads.'

'Only mine,' groaned Jock. 'I've got a head like a foot.'

'Get to sleep mard-arse,' said King. 'Tomorrow is another day. We've got to find the granny with a pogo stick.'

'Oh God, where'd you hear that one?'

'In the gents,' said King, smiling to himself in the dark. 'You've got to learn to listen chum.'

Tomorrow WAS another day. But Jock wasn't that enthusiastic about it.

'Just take me over that stone wall and shoot me,' he pleaded.

'It's not that easy,' said King. 'You can't go around shooting people behind stone walls when you have to find grannies with pogo sticks.'

'Suppose not,' groaned Jock. 'Just make me a coffee pal.'

'Well, I think that's oiled something,' said Jock, emerging from the shower. 'How did we ever have the stamina to be beer reps?'

'Good question,' said King. 'Look, I've just written

yesterday up and I'm going over to the pub to file. Then we're off on the trail again.'

'Oh God!' said Jock. 'Trail! Who do you think I am, the man John Wayne?'

King spoke to Keith Harris, briefly, and said: 'I'm off now, got to meet a granny who goes shopping on a pogo stick.'

'Sometimes I wonder if you're making these up,' said Harris. 'Don't know why we ever had district men or paid freelances. They never seemed to find 'em, Not like this.'

'This is nothing,' said King. 'I met a bloke in the bar last night who thought a stretch-limo was a tandem!'

'Gercha,' laughed Harris, putting down the phone.

Jock joined King as he put the phone down and they went in for a breakfast. 'I don't think I could face a deal this morning,' grumbled Jock, who still looked pale.

King ordered the whole shebang and wolfed it down.

'Away man,' said Jock. 'Let's get a fresh of breath air.'

'You what?' King asked his chum. But he had already left for the car park. King said his farewells to Jackie, who had been down early to do their breakfasts, and said: 'May see you on the way back love. Not far now.'

'Hell, you sound like Captain Scott,' she grinned.

They got the show back on the road. King continued to drive. Jock unusually was quiet. He belched loudly on a narrow bend and said: 'Oops, I beg your pardon.'

King startled by the sudden noise countered: 'Early for the corncrake.' And drove on. Their route took them through Bolton on Swale, Streetham and Danby Wiske. Then they found the turning to the village they were looking for. As they parked up before eleven, there was nowhere to go. 'Let's have a walk, Jock,' said King, to his white-faced chum.

'Good idea. I feel bloody dreadful. What the heck did we get up to last night?'

'A bit of this and that,' grinned King. 'Get some air in your lungs man.'

'Aye, and I'm going to have a stiff port and brandy when the Boot opens.'

110

'Best thing for you,' said his pal. 'But don't forget we've to find a granny.'

The pair walked half a mile up a stony track and back down to the village. 'That's better,' said Jock. The colour had returned to his cheeks.

They stopped outside the old stone building which was just opening for business. 'I love the rattling of the bolts ceremony,' said King. 'You get a sort of comfortable feeling, a bit of security, when you know the pubs are open. Else it's like Sunday. Tongue out and nowhere to go.'

The landlady was already decked out. Looked like a Paris model. 'My God, you two are on time,' she joked. 'Is it a drink you'll be wanting or are you from the insurance?'

'Drink please,' said King. 'I haven't brought my claims forms. I'll have a half of lager and Rob Roy here'll have a port and brandy.'

'Oh, one of those, was it,' the auburn-haired pleasant lady laughed. 'We get a few of those round here. You travelling?'

'Bit of a holiday, bit of working. I'm doing a bit of casual reporting for a paper back home. Looking for the unusual, you know.'

'I know,' she said. 'We have a few unusual ones come in here.'

'Really?' said King, suddenly interested. 'At the moment we're looking for an old dear with a pogo stick.'

He suddenly felt daft saying it.

'Oh, that'll be Granny Croston,' said the landlady. 'She's a right character. She lives across there at the cottage next to the shop,' she pointed to small white-painted cottage. 'Pretty sprightly for her age.'

'She doesn't really have a pogo stick?' asked King.

'She sure does,' said the licensee. 'I reckon if she'd had it 10 years ago she'd have been doing somersaults on it by now. She'll be in at lunchtime. You staying?'

'We've got a camper,' said King for the umpteenth time.

'I'm Becky. Stick it round the back. When you've seen Granny Croston come back and I'll tell you about Bumbly Bernard.'

'Oh Christ,' said Jock. 'Give me another of these. I don't know how I got into this mess.'

They all laughed. King sank his drink and ordered another half. He needed it too. But he wasn't going to let Jock know.

'You might think I'm dressed up for this time of the day,' said Becky. 'Sorry, what do they call you?'

'All sorts of things,' groaned Jock. 'But I'm Jock and this is Joe.'

'Well,' said Becky. 'We had a bit of a commotion in the night. The lads were slow to leave. It's that bloody Karaoke, you know. All think they're Buddy Holly.

'Anyway, things got a wee bit out of hand when the gang on their way home from the Ferret saw we were still open and gate crashed.

'I'm on my own here since Fergie left, and the local lads sort of keep a friendly eye on me. We decided the Ferret lot should leave. They did – but only after a bit of 'persuading'. So I've smartened up early today because I understand the local inspector of law and order is on his rounds. He might just have got to hear about last night's little dust up, so I want both myself and the pub to look ultra-respectable.'

'Everything looks just fine,' said King. 'What time does Granny Croston get in?'

'Noon on the dot for her two milk stouts. I guess it's what keeps her so active.'

'And who's Bumbly Bernie?' asked Jock.

'Now there's another story,' laughed Becky. 'I'll point them out when they arrive. He's got a trick. The two are very funny, but never laugh. Bit like Laurel and Hardy.

'Hey up, here comes Granny Croston now.'

'At least she's walking and not playing Skippy,' said King. 'And she doesn't look that old for a Granny.'

'She's not,' said Becky. 'Had her brood early and went on to enjoy herself even after her poor old Harold died. She'll be early sixties I suppose.'

The trim figure was wearing slacks and a cardigan. She nodded at the two friends and ordered her milk stout. 'Still a

112

bit of east in that wind,' she said. 'You staying?'

King thought it easier to tell a white lie. 'Just overnight. Actually we're reporters for the Evening Press and we're crossing the country. We're looking round the villages for characters and we heard there was a lady here who went shopping on a pogo stick!'

The old dear laughed. 'That'll be me. But it's been done by the local paper God knows how many times. The Gleaner'll give you a picture if you want one. I was bought the damned thing as a joke because I was slowing up with a bit of arthritis. I used to play bowls and go fell walking. When I packed up they said: "She's got to have SOME exercise and one of the bowlers was in town when he spotted this thing in a sports shop window and bought it me. They all thought I'd give it the grandchildren. But I thought "To hell, I'll show 'em".

'After a bit of practice in the back yard I waited until fête day when there were a lot of people about, and bounced out of the cottage like a rubber ball. You should have seen them! As for going shopping on it well, the shop's only next door and the local rag got me in action outside it clinging on to a shopping bag. All a bit of fun really. But I still use it to keep fit,' she laughed. She sank her second bottle of stout and said to the lads: 'Come on over, I'll show you.'

They trailed after her and from the white-washed porch of the little cottage she produced the stick, rather like a colonel selecting his walking stick from the umbrella stand.

Granny Croston walked down to the lane outside, jumped onto the footplates and bounded off down the road. Without stopping she turned after about 40 yards and pulled up alongside the two amazed pals.

Not knowing quite what to say, the pair clapped. 'Do you mind telling me how old you are?' asked King.

'I'm 64 chuck, but I've been known as "Granny" for about 20 years ever since our Louise gave birth. Did you like that? Only thing is I can't do wheelies,' she chuckled.

'Shouldn't you be wearing a jump suit?' asked Jock inanely.

'Away with you. Make of it what you will.'

'What's your first name anyway?' asked King.

'Genevieve,' she answered.

'Jumping Genevieve,' joked King. 'I can dress this up a bit. I'll send you a copy of the paper and they'll get the picture wired from the Gleaner. Tara love.'

The pair went back across to the pub. There was still no sight of the inspector. They had just settled at the bar when a middle-aged couple walked in. The female half looked a right haridan wearing a checked overcoat and a ridiculous hat with a net attached, which looked as if it was usually worn to go to women's meetings, or whist drives. Her man was a wiry little chap wearing cavalry twill trousers, heavy well-polished brogues, a brown hacking jacket and an evil grin.

She sat by the fire, which was still lit daily, more for pleasure than necessity. 'Pint of bitter and a babycham please,' said the cheeky-looking newcomer, who looked about 45. 'And I'll have a look at the menu please.'

'He says that every day,' said his wife. 'He knows damned well what's on it. And I know what he's going to say next. I'll have the crocodile sandwiches, and make it snappy. She'll have the tongue then she can wag both of them all day. He never fails, our Bernard,' said his wife with resignation. 'I think I'm going to have him landscaped. He read debility at Oxford, you know.'

Becky took no notice. She nodded to King and said: 'You'll have realised that's them,' she mouthed. 'Two steak and kidney, is it Bernard?' she asked with assurance.

'Yes please love,' said the wife, who turned out to be Tessa Turner. 'His problem is that he's not got the appropriate requirement between his ears.'

'Have you ever thought how much space women take up in pubs?' asked Bernard pensively.

Tessa ignored him and realising she had the attention of King and Jock she said: 'You'll not have heard of his bumbly bee games then?'

Feigning surprise, King said: 'Bumbly bee games?'

Tessa continued: 'And him making the washing machine

salesman join the Tufty Club the other night. Felt right embarrassed, I did.'

Jock was beginning to feel better. The port and brandy, the fresh air and now this had relit his fuse.

'Let me tell you a story. I swear it's true,' said Tessa. 'He has this bumble bee suit he bought at the white elephant stall at last summer's fête. Some nights he puts it on and startles passers-by. It goes from his neck to the top of his legs. The thing has a headpiece with big eyes and two antennae. And he wears wellies. Really he got it for the kids' Christmas show, but it's got out of hand.

'He was at a darts match when the washing machine man I had called, arrived. He gave me a demonstration, doing my sheets and pillow cases. I said I'd have it, but he wouldn't accept my cheque for some reason. He said it had to be signed for by the man of the house. Of course Bernard here didn't turn up.'

King looked at the neat little chap who was smiling happily into his tankard.

'The poor bloke washed everything in the house. I rang the pub, but they were playing away and then some of them were going off for a game of cards.'

Throughout this tirade Bernard's face never changed. He ordered another and said innocently: 'Another one my little angel, or something different?'

Tessa went on: 'When he eventually got home I explained all he had to do was sign a cheque and the poor bloke could go home.

'I suspect Bernard had had a pop or two more than he is normally accustomed to. He just looked at the harassed salesman and said: "I'll sign the cheque if you'll play bumbly bees." This little fellow, looking at the end of his rope said: "You what?"

'I was getting a little tetchy by this time, and I actually visibly cringed when Bernard said: "Bumbly bees, old sport. All you have to do is put on this suit and mask, my wellies and run round the block. You can change in the lounge!"

'I could see the mood he was in and said to the bloke: "Just do it. It's dark". He looked at me as if he was in the home for the confused. "Are you serious?"

'I told him buggerlugs here was and if he wanted his cheque he'd do it. Bernie the Bolt had just had enough to be awkward. The poor salesman looked at me all helpless like and said something like: "Let's get on with it".

'Bernard leads him to the front door and only tells the poor little sod: "Oh yes. Almost forgot, you have to flap your elbows up and down and say buzz, buzz, buzz all the way round".

'Well, you can imagine once the little fellow had left, our Bernie here came in for some. And how! But he was waiting at the front door for the salesman to return. I often wonder what he told his wife. When he got back all flushed, out of breath and feeling silly, he said: "I met a man with a dog. The dog took one look and scarpered".

'I told him: "Go and take that damned thing off and get dressed". He came back through to the kitchen in his suit and holding the agreement papers and guarantee.'

By now the two friends were convulsed. Jock was wheezing again.

'But that's not all,' said Tessa. She was warming to her obviously well-told story by now. 'Do you know what Bernard said to him? I still don't believe it. He said: "There's just the Tufty Club now". I though the chap was going to pass out.

'I told Bernard: "You're bloody barmy, you are". He just smiled and said to the red-faced salesman: "Join the Tufty Club and the cheque is yours. Honest".

'By now it's midnight, and he has to get back to Richmond. At least he hadn't had time for a drink,' said Tessa almost smiling.

'Little Arkwright, that was the salesman's name, had glazed eyes by now – without having partaken anything stronger than a coffee. He said: "What in God's name is the Tufty Club?"

'So clever breeches here says: "I was in the Pied Bull when a policeman came in with some leaflets about junior road safety.

All club members get a wall-poster about how to cross the road and a little lapel badge.

'Yes, I'll have another please,' said Tessa, obviously parched with the passion of her story. 'Well, little Arkwright was almost manic by now. "I know how to cross the sodding road", he said. And our Bernie here says: "Aye lad, but you haven't got a little badge".

'The outcome was he became a member of the Tufty Club and got his cheque. But I'll never be able to go in their shop again. I'd be too embarrassed.'

King, Jock and Becky were laughing heartily as the landlady went to get the two steak and kidney pies.

King asked tentatively: 'Good tale that Bernard. Tell me, do you do anything else in your bumbly bee suit?'

'Going hand gliding off Beacon Hill tomorrow,' he replied without a flicker. 'Should be good for a laugh.'

The two pals stared at him. They were getting as baffled as the washing machine salesman.

'No, I've got to come clean old man,' said Bernard, who had yet to laugh while all around him roared. 'I'm doing it for charity. It's nothing too big and it's a bit of a hobby.'

'Straight?' said King. 'Look, I'm doing some pieces about local fun and laughter for a paper over on the west. Do you mind me using this story – and getting a picture of you in the morning?'

'Not a bit,' said Bernard. 'It could make me famous. I won't be in the Bahamas at Christmas, but it'll help keep the lifeboats afloat. I do everything for the RNLI.'

'What do you do for a day job?' asked King.

'Play silly beggars,' said Bernard. 'No, seriously I came into a bit of family cash and opted out of the rat-race. It's wonderful to be able to leave it to the rats.'

'Is this green hill far away?' asked King. 'I'll fix up a photographer. What time and where shall we meet you?'

'Eleven at the Bluebell which is on the way. Becky'll show you on the map. And don't worry old boy, you won't have to go up.'

The pair finished their meal and left. Joe asked Becky: 'Are those two for real?'

'They are,' she said. 'We get that story about once a month, but it still makes everyone laugh. If you want to stay the night here in your caravan, I'll do you a meal.'

The couple did. They spent a quiet evening playing darts with a couple of lads from the village. In the morning they set off in good time and arrived at the Bluebell smack on the dot. The photographer was waiting for them.

14

The trio went into the pub. The photographer introduced himself to Jock. It was Pete, who had done the pictures with the wartime pilot.

'I sent Biggles a couple of prints,' he said. 'What is it you're up to now?'

'A bit of hang-gliding,' said King, smiling to himself.

'Not with that old boy again?'

'No, a bumble bee,' said King. This brought no response from Pete who though he was just being facetious.

The landlord of the Bluebell was a large cheerful chap. His red eyes matched his nose. He looked like an ex-boxer, ready to join in the fun – but take no nonsense. 'By gum, you lot are early. We don't usually get many for the bolt-drawing ritual.'

'We're ready for one and meeting someone,' said King, who had left the camper at the side of the pub. Pete put down his heavy metal camera case.

'Just a half please, got a long day,' he said. Weddings, golden weddings, silver weddings. Still, it's better than sitting outside some royal love nest for days on end and then joining in a 30 second scrap for the one picture with about 60 others. I even carry my own two champagne glasses, Woolworth's of course, and an ever-empty bottle for the statutory snap of the old couple. They rarely have more than a cup of tea. Where are we going anyway?'

'Up to Beacon fell to watch a bit of hang-gliding. You'll find out soon enough.' Pete looked at him suspiciously.

The landlord turned out to be Dennis Barber, a former light heavyweight of some fame 20 years ago. This was confirmed by a selection of framed pictures around the old-fashioned public bar. He was now definitely heavyweight.

'Interested in boxing?' asked Dennis.

'A bit,' said Jock.

'No,' said King, as the jovial publican polished the already gleaming pumps. He glanced up as a white transit van drew up outside the window. Then he did a double take.

'Jesus bloody Christ,' he exploded, his eyes widening in horror.

The three turned to behold an amazing scene. There was this slight figure marching across the car park towards the front door. It was wearing a bumble bee head with two huge eyes and a hairy face. It had two antennae wafting on the breeze from the top of its head.

The body was clad in a sort of black and yellow striped padded vest from which two little white, thin legs appeared to dangle. It was shod in turned-down black wellies with thick white seaman's socks turned over their tops. It was an amazing sight to behold in the Yorkshire moors. The snapper and the pugilist stood open mouthed. King and Jock, having had some warning what to expect just heaved with laughter.

The apparition walked into the bar and said politely: 'What ho gentlemen,' as you do.

The ex-boxer, used to being gob-smacked, spluttered: 'Can I help you?'

'Indeed you can,' said Bernard. 'I'll have half of Guinness and a straw. Damned clumsy thing, this mask. Take one for yourself and a quid for the Lifeboat box.' He offered a fiver. Jock declined a second half on account of his aching stomach. King accepted.

'What are you?' gasped the landlord.

'I'm Bumbly Bernard and I'm going hang-gliding with these gentlemen.'

'Ask a silly question . . .'

Dennis served him and went through to fetch his wife. King wondered what he was telling her. Probably something like: 'Don't be startled love, but there's a man-sized, hang-gliding bumble bee drinking Guinness through a straw in the public bar!'

When he returned and his stunned wife had had her peep through the hatch, which she promptly closed, King had recovered sufficiently to tell them all what was going on.

'He simply tots up his air miles, and collects from his sponsors in two or three pubs and at the British Legion,' he said. 'It's all a gimmick to raise cash for the RNLI.'

Dennis was still taking it in when the four left. 'I'll go up in my van with the gear and one of you can bring it down to pick me up. Should be good today. Nice breeze,' said the intrepid Bernard.

'Okay,' said King. 'Run him up Jock. We'll sort it out at the top. Got everything you need Bernard?'

'Certainly old boy. Just follow us in your caravan. The final track's a bit bumpy, but you'll be alright.'

It was about 10 miles from the village before they stopped. Bernard got out and the sheep gazed with as much interest as they could muster.

He unloaded his gear from the back of his van. Even the sail of the craft was black and yellow. He assembled it expertly and prepared for take-off. Holding up wetted finger he surveyed the landscape below. 'I should end up down there by that farm,' he said, pointing the finger. 'Just a nice little blow. About three miles on the map. You good for a quid a piece per mile?'

The trio could only nod. Pete was busy snapping the scene. King and Jock just gazed at the scene in disbelief.

'Well chaps, must miss the TV booster station, chocks away. Here goes. Buzz-buzz, buzz-buzz.' And with one mighty bound he soared into the air. The wind snatched at the sail making a sort of ripping noise like a kite on a beach. 'Well I'm buggered,' said Pete, looking at the other two. 'If I don't get that last shot in the Sunday Times Colour Mag I deserve shooting.'

The trio watched Bernard soaring, and then he dipped his left wing like a fighter pilot who had just spotted a bandit at ten o'clock. Suddenly there was a shriek and then a scream. As the bumble bee dipped out of sight over the escarpment, four elderly hill walkers were just having a flask of coffee.

One of the two women was wailing loudly and set off at a rare gallop down the hill. Their dog whined and shot off in the other direction, clearing a stone wall in one leap and headed for the opposite horizon.

King turned to see Jock rolling in the coarse, wind-swept grass clutching his stomach, unable to breath for laughter.

King took it on himself to pick up the course of the glider when it came back into view. It was heading for the farm as forecast. 'Pete, you take the old boy's van down there. I'll take Jock,' said King. He bundled his mate into the camper and the wagons rolled down the hill.

Towards the bottom a hysterical figure in a head scarf and wearing a blue anorak shot across the lane in front of them. 'She's never going to be believed at the women's circle meeting,' grinned King.

And lo and behold in the field next to the indicated farm was Bernard dismantling his flying machine. 'Bang on, old boy,' he said. 'Super flight and a few more bob in the kitty for the brave boys of the briny. Now, let's got and have a stiffener. My legs are getting chapped.'

Jock joked: 'I don't know about your legs, my brain's getting chapped. Whenever did you see such a fine wee thing zooming through the air? Just as well you didn't have an engine on it Bernard, or we'd never have found you.'

The jaunty little chap replied, taking off Jock's accent: 'Dinnae fash yoursen, wee man. That's next. I'm toying with the idea of investing in a microlite, pretty much the same as this, but wi' a wee motor.'

Dennis stared at him. 'Where did you get the idea in the first place?' he asked.

'After I took early retirement I wanted a hobby, and didn't really feel ready for afternoon bowls with the wrinklies. I find walking boring and I'm past cricket. I have a chum who likes this hang-gliding. He persuaded me to have a go. You start by running off little hills and when you get the hang of it, pardon the pun, you go higher. Then you get confident and go off on your own.

'I had this daft outfit and decided to do it for the Lifeboat. It's just taken off from there. It keeps me fit, I'm only 46 and the locals are most generous. Either that or they think I'm completely barmy and they're paying me protection money. Must be off. Make a decent job of it old boy,' he said to King. 'Oh, I think you owe me a quid a piece.'

The lads stumped up and King said: 'Thanks for the tale Bernard. Good luck in your cause. I'll send you a copy of the paper.'

Pete left for his dark room while King and Jock had a sandwich and a laugh with the ex-boxer and went for a walk before returning to the Pied Bull.

'See you again lads,' he said. 'As I always say, you never know what you'll come across in this trade. Gliding man-sized bumble bees. Get Pete to send up a picture to put on the bar wall will you?'

King and Jock reported back to Becky. She was still well-turned out and smiling. 'The inspector's been and every- thing's fine. I can renew my licence at the Brewsters Sessions next week; Steak and Kidney pie on the house tonight lads.'

The chums went back to the camper. 'I'm knackered,' said Jock. 'Give us that map mate, it'll send me to sleep.' As he studied the Ordnance sheet he started snoring. King wrote up his stuff.

At opening time the weary twosome went back to the bar. 'Tired but happy, that's me,' commented King. 'I've never had so much fun. Think of all the years we spent round those dismal pubs Jock. I could get used to this.'

He left Jock chatting to the amiable Becky and went into the passage to ring Maggie on the pay-phone. 'How are you doing love?' She asked. She always asked that first with concern in her voice. 'You're getting bags of stuff in the paper. What have you been up to today?'

'Oh, nothing much,' chuckled King. 'A granny on a pogo stick and a hang-gliding bumble bee.'

'Oh yeah! I believe that when I see it.'

'You will,' promised Jock. 'Kids okay?'

'Just fine. Cunliffe's have been round again looking for your company car. Obviously they've seen your pieces in the Press and they think you've gone off in their Sierra.'

'I must get a bit about the camper in this piece then,' said King to his wife. 'I may not be able to use the car again, but they can't flog it while it's hidden. They may even forget it in time!'

'Fat chance of that. You don't improve with age.'

'I'll plead insanity brought on by the shock of losing my job.'

'When are you coming home?'

'Only a few days now. Jock can't take much more,' he laughed.

'And I shouldn't think you can either, you old ale can,' chuckled Maggie. 'Try to hurry it up. The kids are asking who you are!'

The lads had their free steak and kidney pies and went for an early night. They both had a shower and washed some clothes, hanging them on a line over the stove. As King sat to check through his piece again he said to his mate: 'It's a long time since I've had to do my own dhobi-ing.'

'Can't ever remember doing it in my life,' said Jock. 'Couldn't we find one of those washing machine places where they do it for you?'

'Up here?' King looked at his pal. 'Like a Chinese take-away too?'

He filed bang on time in the morning and got through to Harris on the news desk. 'It's just dropped. Great stuff,' he said. 'How long can you keep it up, Joe?'

'I'm beginning to enjoy myself. But I've no plans for today yet, so it's out into the void. Still, you've a few in the can. I'll come across something. Should be finished in about three days, Keith. I'm running a bit short of exes. I could do with some readies.'

'Can you cash a cheque in a pub or something. You'll get it back. But from where you are on the map there are only village post offices. If you can hold out until the coast, I'll wire you some. Where shall I send it?'

King glanced at his map and admitted: 'It's a bit bloody remote up here. It'll have to be Whitby. I'm sure the lass here'll cash me one to see me through.'

'It'll be at Whitby General in two days,' said Harris. 'Don't forget to take your driving licence as ID. Good luck today. Incidentally, are you sure about this hang-gliding bee? It's a bit far fetched.'

'I was there,' said King. 'The pix should have been wired to you by now.'

There was a brief silence and Harris returned to the phone. 'Good God, man. I've got them here. They were still in the wire room basket from overnight. This is one hell of a picture story. I've got the editor standing here. He's almost wetting himself. Keep it up matey. Talk to you in the morning.'

Jock had just finished his breakfast, looking a lot better than the previous day. Becky brought King his personal feast and another pot of tea. King settled up and said to her: 'Don't like to ask love, but there's a shortage of banks around here. Can you cash me a cheque? I've got a back up card.'

'Of course I will. And there's no need for cards.'

'Thanks,' said King. 'Look, we're running short of ideas, dream us something up, something daft that you know of between here and the coast. I'll give you a ring tonight. And with a bit of luck when we're through we can break off and come in for a quickie.'

'Take care and keep laughing,' said Becky as the pair drove off into the rising sun.

'You know, I could fall in love with her,' said Jock.

'There's some grand folk up here. Still, I suppose we are a bit nearer Scotland,' King answered with a telling glance.

Once again the two were not far adrift from the path along which crusty old Wainwright had led thousands of fervent followers over the years, each of them clutching his beautifully hand-written and hand-drawn pocket guide.

'He was treasurer of Kendal council,' said King. 'Turned out to be the pied piper of the fells.'

They parked up mid-morning for another read of the map

and a perusal of Wainwright's guide which, incredibly, was first published in 1973. 'I don't know about a pied piper, the man was a magician with his black pen,' said Jock. 'Let's leave the wheels here and go for a walk. Come on buddy, you never know.'

'Looks a bit quiet to me Jock,' said King. 'We need something today.' It was another remote but pretty village with two pubs and a church. 'At least they've got the balance right,' laughed King. 'Do you know, when we go on from here we actually head across Great Fryup Dale into Glaisdale and then Eskdale.'

The east wind still had a knife in it which they noticed after the warmth of the van. The pubs were on either side of the village green. Jock began to take more interest in life. 'Let's have a walk first,' said King. 'Then we'll stand in the middle and toss a coin.'

'Great Fryup Dale, did you say?' asked Jock, his brain grinding into motion with the help of the strong air. 'That's just what I fancy. And what's this tossing up business. Can't we go to them both? Try one each even.'

After a 20 minute stroll the pair stood on the green. 'It's the White Horse or the Red Lion,' said King. 'Let's go for the horse.'

As they strolled towards the granite inn Jock suddenly grabbed King's arm and said: 'I think you're a right jammy sod.'

'You what?' asked King, bemused.

A strange figure in a belted gabardine mac was shuffling towards the Red Lion, his right hand raised stiffly as if asking the teacher if he could leave the room.

The pair did a smart turn about and King offered a polite: 'Good morning. Still fresh.'

The figure turned and the face was not nearly so old as his shuffle. It looked as if it had had a battering at some time. Perhaps another boxer, thought King. Keeping his hand stiffly in the air, the man replied: 'Jesus wants me for a sunbeam.'

King heard Jock's intake of breath and said: 'A bit thin on sunbeams, is he?' He immediately regretted having been flippant to one who was obviously one of life's unfortunates.

'Mock thee not,' said the man, who was much larger than he had seemed ambling, slack-shouldered across the green. 'Always remember a rolling greenhouse shouldn't throw stones.'

King could hear Jock snortling to his left. He said to the man: 'You appear to be about to enter this public house.'

The figure walked on towards the central door to the Red Lion. With his arm raised so stiffly he couldn't get through the aperture. So, keeping his arm thus, he bent his knees and scraped through by his fingernails.

They followed him into the bar and a fresh faced young man said: 'Morning Mike. Everything okay today?'

'Usual please.'

The two waited with bated breath. Surely Jesus's intended sunbeam wasn't about to swill down a pint of bitter. The barman poured him an orange cordial as he went to sit in the window seat, arm still raised stiffly above him as if in an exaggerated Nazi salute.

He quaffed his drink in one and the arm dropped with a hefty slam onto the table with a thud that alarmed Jock who was just ordering.

'King whispered to the barman: 'Is he okay?'

'Not exactly. He used to be Yorkshire's best tight head prop forward. He's Mike Morrell.'

'Gerrout,' said King. He remembered the name from his own days in local rugger. 'What on earth's the matter with him?'

'Kick on the head against Cumberland. Fractured skull. Four weeks in a coma. Hospital nine months. Sent home. Bingo!'

'Can he talk about it? I'm a sports reporter from the Evening Press,' lied King. 'I wondered what had happened to Morrell. He seems to have turned to God.'

'I don't think he knows which way he's turned. What's your name?'

'King, Joe King.' said King, receiving from the young landlord the sort of look he had long been used to.

'I'm Arnie Barratt. Howdo. Poor old Mike used to really be one of the lads. If you want I'll introduce you. Don't expect too much.'

He walked round the bar to the pathetic figure staring at his empty glass and said: 'Mike, this is Joe. He's a sports reporter. Do you mind having a word with him?'

Jock stayed at the bar. King sat next to the ruined young man. 'I'm from Lancashire, Mike,' he said. 'How you feeling these days?'

'Played against Lancashire at Liverpool. I think they called it Blundellsands,' he said, haltingly.

'Kick on the head and unconscious. Now I just walk about. I talk to God about my terrible headaches.'

'You'll be alright soon,' said King, not knowing really what to say. 'You have a walk every day, do you?'

But he'd got all he was getting. The eyes went vacant again. 'Good luck pal,' said King, relieved to return to the bar. He was saddened by what he had seen.

It must have shown. 'Come on man,' said Jock. 'They can't all be witty nut cases you know. There are two sides to life.' Looking at Barratt between the bar pumps, he said: 'What's he do all day?'

'Wanders around. He doesn't know whether it's Christmas Eve or Marble Arch. not even the specialists know why he sticks his arm up. Perhaps it's some sort of unconscious protection after the injury he suffered. He lives with his mum, Winnie, who does a bit of cleaning here. The villages had a good whip round for him and the locals organise things for him.

'He has his Social Security and there was a good pay out from the Rugby Union's insurance. So he's okay financially. I don't mind when he forgets to pay for his glass of pop. It's just sad to see such a great sportsman like that.'

The pair finished their halves and left. 'I feel bloody depressed now Jock,' said King. 'Let's get out of this place.'

'Like I said Joe, there are two sides to life. So far we've only encountered the light-hearted. It doesn't work that way.

They can't all be fooling around and making us laugh. You came on this trip to find characters. You've just found one.'

'True,' said King. 'I'll give the desk a ring at our next stop and see if they want the sad bits too. I could write a piece like: "Mike Morrell, the tough guy Yorky forward destined for an England call-up is spending his days in a haze on a moorland village in North Yorkshire". That sort of thing.'

They crossed the high moorland which looked cold and bleak. There was the odd hill farm. It was land where the farmers and their sheep where nail-tough. The breeze was making the tussock grass look like moving water. Half a mile or so short of Glaisdale they stopped in a reservoir car park and walked into the village. It had a new housing estate, and a church but they didn't have to work hard to find a pub.

'Well, there's a church, any road up,' said King. 'Where there's a church you'll always find a pub.' There were, in fact three, in the little village. The church had a pointed spire atop its tower. Tucked down on the river, the village had a steep main street and high moors all round. It even had a railway station, where the train would take you to chemical Middlesborough. But there was no bus service.

It was again a toss up which to go into. 'This'll do,' said Jock. 'I've had enough of this walking business. The glasses and the brasses gleamed, the food smelled appetising and Jock spotted the name of his favourite lager on one of the old pumps.

'This'll do for a while, Jock,' said King. 'Get 'em in while I ring the office.' He got straight through to Harris, using a transfer charge call to the switchboard. He told him the tale of Mike Morrell.

'Of course we'll use it,' said Harris. 'After all, it's human interest we're looking for. Bung it over marked for my attention and I'll talk to you usual time in the morning. Have the rest of the day off,' he joked.

'Day off?' laughed King. 'It's been one long day off since I set off. I just want to get back on the trail of nonsense not gloom. See you.'

Neither of the lads felt very jolly. King returned from the

129

phone and they had another lager and decided against a bar snack. 'We've been eating and drinking for what seems months,' said Jock, who was beginning to look weather-beaten and ring rusty.

'Let's go back to the van and I'll write up the Morrell piece and we'll see how we feel tonight,' suggested King. 'Then if we want we can have a drive down here and see if there's any action. After all, Keith told me to take the rest of the day off.'

The pair left the homely pub and King suggested: 'We need a blow. Let's take a look at the Beggar's Bridge over the river Esk and then head back for the van.'

'What's the Beggar's Bridge?' asked Jock.

'A seventeenth century stone bridge,' said King. 'And that's a long time mate.' The couple walked under the old railway track and came upon the three hundred year old bridge. They stood admiring the wonders of the old architecture, filling their lungs with good air.

'I can almost smell the sea in it,' said King. 'It's not far in a straight line.' And they strolled back to the camper, both treating themselves to yet another postcard. 'Got to keep a record of the voyage,' laughed Jock.

'That's better mate, laugh,' said King. 'This air is what we've been lacking. Too much time in smoky tap rooms eating steak pie and chips. Come on, lets get back home and get a few words on paper.'

That evening they drifted into town in the camper and returned to the pub where they'd had their morning drink. But neither seemed to have the heart for a hoolie, and action seemed thin on the ground. 'Tomorrow's another day,' said King. 'Let's call it a night. We'll go off in search of fun and laughter in the morning.'

15

The next morning was actually sunny. At his appointed time King filed his piece. A lass on the switchboard complained: 'A bit morose for you, this, Joe,' she said. 'No bumble bees or dogs on wheels?'

'Fresh out of those today,' laughed King. 'But it's better than nowt. Give me Keith on the desk love.'

The news editor asked: 'Where today, Joe? We could do with another couple of daft ones before you come home.'

'Towards the coast. A few miles to go yet,' answered King. They drove a mile or two east and King pulled off, to examine his map.

'Let's give this a go, Jock,' he said, pointing to a village on the Ordnance sheet. 'Looks as if it could be lively. If it's not we'll have a day in Whitby. Keith said my exes have been wired through. So we have to get those either today or tomorrow.'

The village was not exactly busy, but there was a presence around the couple of shops – enough folk on the two streets to make a decent party. Trouble was, there was no party. There was a pub and a church and a village hall. And it was at the village hall rather than the pub, for once, that attracted the attention of the two adventurers.

For in the village shop was a notice which said simply:

> Beetle racing,
> Thursday, 7.30pm.
> Organised by the Young Farmers Club.
> In aid of Mencap.

'Is that some sort of joke?' asked Jock.

'Let's find out,' suggested King. They entered the shop, old fashioned smells like chamois leather, mothballs and paraffin floated from one side. On the other side there were fresh rolls and cold meats in a glass refrigeration case. Toffees were for sale in old fashioned jars. Nothing appeared pre-packed.

A weathered tinkling bell above the door attracted a similarly old-fashioned woman from the back room. She had grey hair and wore an old full-length apron without sleeves. She was wearing a woollen cardigan beneath it, lisle stockings and modern trainers, her only concession to the world of today.

'Take no notice of this bit of sun,' she said suspiciously, 'it could be siling down by toneet.'

King could imagine Wilfred Pickles in the village, presenting a bit of homely fun from the people to the people! Or Brian Johnston doing a Down Your Way from the shop with his old fashioned BBC mike.

'Good morning,' said King. 'Er, I'll have a quarter of those mints please.'

'I'm Martha,' said the old dear. 'I were born in't room above here,' she inclined her head and reached for an old glass jar of mints, and tipping a quota onto her scales. King never got the chance to see if he'd got the full measure. Computer scales had passed this part of the world by on a trek to the smart towns further north.

'That'll be one and a tanner,' said Martha. Then she hurriedly corrected herself: 'I mean 22 pee. Still can't get the hang of this new money.'

Although no mathematician, King knew that one and six was nothing like 22 pence. One and six was seven and a half new pence. Twenty two pence would have been about four shillings and sixpence. He suspected crafty old Martha had, in fact, a very good grasp of currency, both new and old.

Jock was waiting impatiently for his pal to ask the question. He did so.

'Thanks Martha,' he said. 'I wonder if you can help me. We're not from round here . . .'

She cut him dead. 'Then you've missed a lot,' she chuckled. 'All sorts of things go on round here.'

'That's what I was going to ask you,' said King. 'What exactly is beetle racing? Is it a beetle drive, or something?'

She looked at him as if he were barmy. 'Beetle drive! It's not a beetle drive. It's not a whist drive. It's not your dad's front drive. Beetle racing is beetle racing.'

'I saw the notice in your window,' said King.

'There's a lot of notices in my window.' said Martha. 'If you want a mountain bike Billy Cross has his up for sale. The number's on the postcard,' she said, pointing to a host of odd cards and clippings advertising fresh mussels, lawnmower sharpening and a child minding service.

'No, it was the beetle . . .'

She cut him short again. 'Billy wants sixty quid for it so's he can go on the school trip to Munich, but I reckon you'd get it for fifty five. And why they want to take kids to Munich I don't know. That's where that mad Hitler came from.'

'No, he came from . . .' Forget it, thought King. 'Look Martha, I don't really want a mountain bike. I just want to know what beetle racing is.'

'Thirty bob a piece,' said the gnarled old woman. 'Village Hall toneet. In aid of charity. Tickets on sale here.'

'I'll have two,' said King, realising he was getting nowhere. He handed over three pounds and said goodbye. The pair had just tinkled the worn door bell on their way out when Martha bellowed: 'They paint their arses.'

The pair continued their path through the ancient portals and Jock looked at his mate in stunned silence – for once. 'What the hell do you make of that. Is she real?' he gasped.

Jock, feeling a lot better after the previous day's sobriety, had already spotted the pub. 'There's the Octopus and Wardrobe,' he grinned. 'We might get a bit more sanity in there.'

'And a pint of lager, you mean,' laughed King. He could

sense things happening again. They walked into the Arms, and King observed: 'I'll give 'em one thing, they keep their pubs proper-like round here.'

'Aye, a bit better than round Canal Street back there,' said Jock, aiming his thumb behind him in the rough direction from which they had come.

The bar was still empty, but it smelled ready for action. The pumps had been pulled off and there was a tinge of hotpot in the air.

'Morning, what'll you be having this fine day?' demanded a lilting Irish voice.

King started: 'Bloody hell, it's the invisible man again.' Jock was looked round nervously, his hand covering his nigh empty wallet in his back pocket.

Then an impish face grinned over the bar. 'Hope I didn't startle youse me boyos,' he said cheerfully. 'I was just down the cellar.'

King looked over the bar and saw the cellar flap still raised. 'Hope your cooler's OK,' he said, unable to avoid harking back to his dozens of calls at the Roebuck.

'And what'll that be meaning?' asked the Irishman.

'Sorry,' said King. 'It's an old joke. We both used to be brewery reps and every time I see a cellar I go through replacing or having repaired someone's cooling system.'

'And what brewery would that be?' asked the Irishman.

'Cunliffe's,' said King.

'They went busted,' said the Irishman.

'That's why we're here,' said Jock. 'Having a bit of a break to get it out of our systems. A sort of coast to coast pub crawl. What do they call you?'

'Paddy,' said Paddy.

'Ask a daft question,' interjected Jock, keeping a straight face. 'I'm Jock and this is Joe. He's English. So we've almost got a full set.' They all laughed and King bought the beers.

'Having one Paddy,' he asked. 'No tanks, it's a bit early for me,' said the Irishman. 'But perhaps on this occasion oi'll break

134

the habits of a lifetime.' King noticed he had a Bushmills whiskey.

'What is it that brings you to this neck of the moors then?' asked Paddy. 'We're a bit off the beaten track.'

Jock was about to speak when King stepped in: 'Just cruising about for a week or so in search of fun and laughter,' he said, cutting off his mate's reply. 'Tell me Paddy, we've just been to the village store and we saw a notice about Beetle racing. What the hell's that when it's at home?'

'They paints their arses,' said Paddy. He was about to expand on the subject when an Irish brogue came from the kitchen. 'Do you have a minute Patrick?'

The landlord answered the call and Jock said to his buddy: 'What the hell's everyone getting their arses painted for? Why did you stop me explaining what we're up to?'

'Sometimes it's better to be incognito and others it's better to announce yourself formal like,' said King, feigning wisdom and vast editorial experience. 'But I'll tell you one thing chum, we're onto something here. I can feel it in my water.'

Paddy's task could not have been onerous. He was back behind his bar in less than five minutes, and quickly finished his Bushmills. 'And where'll you be heading?' he asked the two travellers.

'The coast,' said King. 'Probably have a day in Whitby, like to see Robin Hood's bay.'

'Tis a wonderful place that,' said Paddy. 'Cliffs tall enough to give yer mother-in-law a slide. Some good little pubs too. One or two on the way as well. Good fish and chips in Whitby.'

'There would be,' said Jock, grinning so as not to appear sarcastic. 'But tell us, who paints whose bums?'

'The farmers,' laughed Paddy, his cheeky face alive after his first drink of the day; or perhaps it wasn't!

'What,' said King, 'the farmers paint each other's bums?'

'No, the beetles,' said Paddy.

'I'm completely confused now,' said King. 'All this bum painting goes on in the village hall.'

'That's right. Only two such events in the whole of England.'

'Where's the other?' said Jock.

'Somewhere in Derbyshire,' said Paddy. ''Tis an amazing sight to see. You'll get tickets at the shop if you're staying in the locality.'

King didn't have the heart to tell him now that they'd already got them. 'Come on Paddy, come clean. What's it all about?'

'Well, the Young Farmers Club, you know, those that do it in wellies, have been holding the event for years. You see they have a special race track, and it's on a big board. The beetles are put in six different glass tubes that fit into lanes, and they put a blob of paint on their bums. All the patrons have a bet. It's a quid a go now. You bet on your colour and the winners go to the 'tote' to collect after it's over. Half the takings go to charity, as do the entrance fees. I shall be doing the licensed bar this year. That was my Colleen telling me to go up the hall after lunch to put the pumps on and take the optics.'

'Is this for real Paddy?' asked King. 'It's not a bit a blarney?'

'Is the Pope a catholic?' grinned the little impish Paddy. 'I swear to God it's true.'

'Does it get Press coverage?' asked King, tentatively. 'I've got a pal on the local paper back home and he'd sure be grateful if I could send him an article.'

'It used to be done in the papers around here, but over the years it's become commonplace and they don't seem to bother any more. In fact the farmers would welcome a bit more attention. It's in aid of Mencap this year.'

'Have you a phone I can use?' asked King. 'It'll be a transfer charge call.'

'Bejasus, I can stand you a phone call,' said the Irishman. 'The instrument is on the other bar, see, through there.'

In spite of his offer, King made his call collect after telling Jock: 'Get 'em in. All three.' Jock did. King took the remnants of his first pint through to the lounge and called the operator. The cheery lass on the switchboard answered: 'Where are you now, Joe?'

'God knows,' said King. 'Up in the hairy mountains. Is Keith on the desk?' He was put through.

'How're you doing Joe? Not struck already? You didn't have an idea at 8.30 this morning.'

'How about painting beetles' bums and racing them. It's the local event of the year. For charity. Starts at 7.30. I've bought a ticket. Organised by the young farmers.'

Harris went quiet for a minute, and King realised he was telling someone what he was now up to. 'Where are you Joe? Is this for real?'

'It is. I'll be there and I'll file at 8.30 as usual in the morning. Sithee.'

The three stood talking, the bar being otherwise empty. 'And other strange customs round here?' asked King, hopefully.

'Not customs, but a fair few strange people,' said the landlord, who appeared to have acquired the taste and bought a round.

'There's Carmen the Foolish, who's a bit mysterious. She was arrested for prowling one night. A woman prowler! Said she was looking for hedgehogs. The court case was a hoot. That attracted a bit of attention in the Press. The prosecuting inspector was asked by the chairman of the magi- strates who the arresting office was. The inspector replied: "Sinbad".

'The silly old sod said: "The sailor?"

'And the officer said: "No, that was the name of the police dog who apprehended the accused". She was given a conditional discharge and told to leave the local wildlife alone. To this day PC Atkinson, the dog handler, is known as Sinbad, among other things. And I thought we were supposed to be daft in Ireland!

'If youse lads want a laugh get down to the hall tonight. Competition is due to start at 7.30, but it never does. The licensed bar opens at seven, but if you knock three times about quarter to, oi'll give you one before the rush.'

Back in the camper King asked his partner in crime: 'What do you make of this?'

'Must be right,' said Jock. 'Or the old dear wouldn't be selling tickets.'

'Damn,' said King. 'I never picked up my one and a tanner mints.'

'Well, it'd be no good going back now, they'll be back in that jar. The old girl must be worth a fortune.'

They presented themselves early as planned, and King knocked three times. Paddy unlocked the door, peered round and ushered them in.

'You don't want me to whisper "love" do you?' asked Jock. It was lost on Paddy, who rebolted the door.

'I've got a special brew on tap. A local beer with a reputation for making sturdy men fall off their bikes on the way home. Fancy one?'

'In for a penny . . .' said King. 'We'll start with a half if it's got meths added!'

They were pulled two halves for which the Irishman asked one pound fifty. And Jock took a swig. 'Jeez, what the hell is this stuff? It'd grow hair on a door knob,' he gasped. 'Tastes more like a spirit than a glass of ale.'

'The brewery does it specially for functions like this,' said Paddy. 'It's done from barrel bottoms, using the yeast and then brewed in the normal way. Apparently they've been doing it for a hundred years. You're only supposed to have two pints.'

'I think this half will do me,' said King. 'Then a nice, harmless lager.'

Prompt at seven, Paddy opened the door of the wooden building, once the local seat of learning venue, for the local council's monthly meeting, where nothing much more than clipping hedges and putting in applications to the Rural District Council for new road signs was discussed.

It was the home for the kids' Christmas party, a fact underlined by bits of coloured crepe bunting still attached to drawing pins in inaccessible corners. They had the New Year hop there, 'When,' said Paddy, 'the special brew came out again.'

After 10 minutes there were some dozen people at the bar, all ordering the special.

By half past there were almost 50 people in the hall. Pints

138

of the special were sliding into well-steaked guts under red noses, honed by the east wind, and young farmers' caps.

'Looks like the action's starting,' said Jock, watching four strapping young men ascend the stage and vanish behind the faded curtain. They reappeared with a strange contraption, a games board you could never buy at Hamlyns.

It was about six foot by four foot wide, divided by plywood into six lanes, each numbered. It was placed on a trestle table in the centre of the hall. Another table had appeared to the right of the stage behind which sat a matronly-looking woman with a florid complexion, chubby cheeks and a broad smile. She looked as if she washed regularly with carbolic and a scrubbing brush. She placed before her six piles of tickets. The excitement was growing with the attendance figure. There must have been seventy people drinking and waiting for the action.

The old curtain twitched and Jock laughed: 'You half expect poor old Tommy Cooper to come out,' he said.

Then the curtain was pulled back by some invisible cord and there stood two figures, and one holding a box, rather like an old cigar box, and a card table on which were six long glass tubes, probably nicked from the nearest secondary school chemistry lab, and an old man, who took centre stage.

The younger man announced: 'Ladies and gentlemen, I'm sure you all know Councillor Joss Pentland.'

King nudged Jock as the councillor put his thumbs in the pockets of his brown waistcoat which was part three of his brown suit.

'Evenin' all,' he said, sounding like Jack Warner in Dixon of Dock Green, except for the accent.

'I welcomes all of you to this year's Beetle Race, the proceeds of which will go towards Mencap.' There was a ripple of applause and a shout of 'Good on yer Joss, me owd lad.' The special was already beginning to tell.

'I declare the event open,' announced Councillor Pentland proudly. A banner above him, which looked as if it had been used for many years, unrolled itself above his head, again

139

operated by a tug from behind the scenes. It unfurled proudly like the last Union Jack over Rangoon.

'I'm sure as what you all knows the rules. Bettin' slips are at Jean's table. It's a quid a ticket. Let's get on with it.' A great roar of approval rent the air. Paddy could not keep up with demand at the bar and had found a colleague to help him.

Councillor Pentland was helped off the stage and the young farmer carried down, more athletically, the cigar box and the glass tubes, which were placed in the lanes on the board.

'There's a funny smell, Jock,' said King. 'It's either Paddy's little legs burning with acceleration, or something's gone off.'

The young farmer turned out to be Bob Whittle, a local landowner since the death of his father, with a gunsmith's shop.

King and his pal got nearer to the action as Bob opened the box. 'Bloody hell,' said King. 'Multi-coloured beetles.'

Bob showed them proudly to the punters. 'As you will see, we are again using the cockroach type of beetle, renowned for their speed over six feet.' This bought more cheers and jeers. And by this time Paddy's optics were going up and down like Tower Bridge.

'And as you will see, they have been painted with the harmless dye used by fishermen on maggots. And now for the bit you all like. Bring it in Sam.' This time there were 'boos' and 'poohs.'

'And as you all know beetles or cockroaches will chase only scents. So we have prepared our usual bits of rotting this and that.' He didn't explain what the 'this and that' was.

'Right Sam, a good blob at the end of each lane if you would be so kind.'

Sam, who looked like a blacksmith, took a tea spoon from his breast pocket and dug out six dollops of the disgusting mixture, placing them at the end of each line. Bob held the tubes up on their closed end and Sam popped a different coloured creature in each. They fell to the bottom in confusion, unable to escape.

'Right ladies and gentlemen, place your bets,' said Councillor Pentland grandly. There was a rush to Jean's table.

140

'Eh, one at a time you lot,' she yelled over the hub-bub.

'What colour do you fancy Jock?' asked King.

'Yellow,' said Jock. 'Oh my God.'

'What's up?' asked his pal!

'Sam's putting the bloody spoon back in his pocket. I hope we're not asked round to tea. I told you there was a funny smell.'

'I'll put your quid in, you get two more halves,' said King.

With the clamour round the 'tote' there was a space at the bar. 'There, I told you so,' grinned Paddy. 'I don't think you believed me.'

'Just give us a couple more,' said Jock. 'I've seen it, but I still don't think I believe it.'

He went back and joined his pal as near the action as they could get, which was about three deep from the track. He asked: 'What colour you on Joe?'

'Blue,' said King.

A neighbour standing next to them in the crush said: 'Blue. That blue bugger's a behemoth.'

'A what moth?' asked King. 'I thought it was a bloody beetle.'

'A behemoth,' said the fellow. 'A monster or huge creature. Old fashioned word.'

'Has it a chance?' enquired King.

'All depends who gets the scent first,' said their companion.

Councillor Pentland demanded: 'Betting over for the first race. Lower the tubes and go.'

The crowd was silenced. All eyes were on the cockroaches. Nothing happened. Then one dyed green got a sniff and set off. It's fellow creatures must have been spurred, for they all set off in pursuit down their private crystal tunnels, and the cheering started. The insects stopped occasionally, and the lads were told: 'That's because of the lights. They usually operate in the dark in their natural habitat But if we did that, nobody would see anything.'

Blue won it by a good three inches, and King went to collect his winnings along with about 20 others. They were all on even money as there had been no research into handicapping racing beetles.

'See, there's nowt to it Jock,' he grinned. 'What now?'

'I can't stand this stink. I think you've got enough for your article. How about a breath of fresh air? Get the phone number of that Bob bloke and ring him early in the morning to find our how much they raised.'

'You're getting the hang of this, Jock,' laughed King. 'How about a cool pint and cod and chips at Paddy's. I saw it on the blackboard.'

'Good thinking,' said Jock, and they fed and watered and returned to the camper for King to do his writing. Tomorrow was another day.

The following morning was bright again. The rain forecast by crafty Martha had stayed away, probably in the Lake District. 'She probably wanted us to buy cagoules,' said King.

He filed his stuff and told the copytaker he'd have a word with Harris after breakfast – which Jock was cooking when he got back to the camper. It was only bacon butties, but Jock remarked: 'I think this is the first time we've done anything for ourselves. Hey mate, can you believe last night?'

'I rang Bob before I put my stuff over and do you know, they made four hundred and fifty quid. Not bad for a bunch of blue-arsed beetles.'

The two strolled down to the phone box together and King got straight through to Harris. 'This is amazing, Joe,' said the news editor. 'Take that day off now. I trust you've no more daft things up your sleeve?'

'Not yet, but I've got to go to Whitby to pick up those expenses. I'll perhaps take it easy and just keep my thingies and wotsists open.'

'Good man. Talk to you in the morning,' said Harris, ringing off.

'Do you know Jock, that poor beggar is stuck to his desk all day. Has to be in at the crack, go through all the nationals, mark up the diary for the reporters, be bored to hell in the morning conference, listening to sales figures and daft ideas

142

from the circulation department. No wonder they call them shiny arses.'

'At least they're not blue,' chuckled Jock. 'How come you know all this anyway?'

'I went in a time or two and had lunch with Keith before I set off into the unknown. Hey, there's Paddy.'

The little pixie of a man was unloading empty metal kegs from the tailboard of his pick-up. 'That was one hell of a night,' he said.

'Even after my percentage to the fund I took enough for a normal week. It got mad towards the end. They couldn't get it down fast enough. Ordering two pints at a time because of the crowd at the bar. Bejasus, I could do with a night or two like that in here. Where's you two off now?'

'Day off in Whitby. A quiet day off,' chortled King. 'And we too have to do a bit of financing.'

'Lovely place Whitby. I love the seaside. Don't try to count the steps up to the old abbey on the cliff. The condition you two look in, they'd need an air-sea chopper to rescue you half way up. I have a good pal there, another Paddy. Paddy O'Neill. He's got the Figurehead down near the water. Anyone will tell you where it is. Tell him I sent you and he'll tell you a good yarn. See you again lads.'

'That sounds a bit ominous for a day off,' said Jock looking somewhat concerned. 'We can't keep this up for much longer.'

'Eh, tha's not weakenin' lad?' laughed King, over-acting the Lancashire dialect.

'You want to get yourself a ukulele and you'd sound like George bloody Formby,' retorted Jock.

'You leave our George out of this,' laughed King. 'He and Tom Finney were my two schoolboy heroes. Oh yes, and Dennis Compton,' he added.

'Come on you soft sod,' said Jock. 'Let's go to the seaside for the day. Then I suppose it's back up here?'

'Sure is,' said King. 'We've got to see this through. Wagons roll.'

The Post Office at Whitby seemed in some disarray. Like

at any general Post Office there seemed too many queues and too many people. The harassed staff were keeping their cool in the face of abuse and confusion. They were dealing with postal orders, TV stamps, telephone stamps, queries about National Savings Certificates, pensions. People were arguing about who was first in which queue. They were like sheep worried by a dog.

'It's like Calcutta railway station,' said King. 'Not that I've ever been further than France, but it's always on those TV travel programmes. At least there's no beggars here.'

King waited his turn patiently, defying the temptation to lane hop as everyone else seemed to be doing. When he reached the window he said to a tired looking young lady: 'My name's King, Joe King.' He immediately regretted it, but she didn't say it!

'I have to collect some cash wired to me from the Evening Press in Lancashire. This is my driving licence.'

The young lady opened a large drawer, extracted an envelope, which obviously contained the authorisation, and counted him out a pile of notes. It was as simple as that.

King pocketed the money without counting it. 'A hundred and eighty smackeroos, Jock,' he gleamed. 'We're safe again for a bit.' He peeled off three tenners and stuck them in his pal's top pocket, grinning. 'That's so's you can keep buying your round. We've only a couple of days to go. Let's have a look round the harbour.'

The couple strolled across the iron swing bridge to the old side of the harbour, the ruins of the ancient abbey looming above them. There were antique shops, home made toffee shops, local jet jewellery shops an old inn and at the end, to the right: The Steps.

Jock looked at him. 'Don't even think about it. Remember what Paddy said. And I think I just heard a helicopter!'

'No steps,' promised his mate. 'It's just lovely to see the briny again. Much as I like the fells and love the folk up there, you do feel you're back in the land of the living down here. What was the name of that pub Paddy told us about?'

'The Figurehead. Fancy one?' The couple sauntered back to the harbour bridge and after five minutes watching the fishing boats, King asked a passer-by. 'It's a fair hike from here mate,' said the local. 'You got a car?'

The pair decided to walk. The Figurehead was on the waterside about half a mile from the sea front.

The pub was half suburbia, half seaside. It still had a fire burning in the old grate in the lounge where the couple settled.

Jock ordered two halves from his new-found wealth from the big, broad shouldered, balding chap behind the bar.

'On holiday, are you?' he asked them, in a now familiar Irish accent.

'Just a few days off. Come across the fells, or do you call them the moors?'

'Call them the bogs if you want,' he chuckled.

'You must be Paddy.'

'Jeez, you're observant if nothing else,' laughed the guvnor.

'Just won Mastermind,' laughed King. 'No, we've been to see your buddy Paddy up there. He told us to come and see you if we'd time. We went beetle racing last night and Paddy certainly has a tale to tell. He told us if we came in here you could out do him any day.'

'What're you selling, buckets of blarney? So you've been to see old Paddy have you? A hell of a character he's been. He was a jockey, you know, back home. But he claimed he was given only donkeys to ride and he could do that on Whitby sands, so he came over here and took a pub in town before moving up to the village.'

'We're a couple of redundant brewery reps from the west coast,' admitted King, feeling Jock looked at him enquiringly. 'Seeing we know the trade, the local evening paper asked us to take a cross country ride and collect a few pub tales.'

Paddy rolled his eyes, poured himself a gold label, and looked steadily at the pair. 'Tales, there's more tales round here than old Aesop could have made up,' he said. 'And these are true.

'I'll give you one for nowt. It happened only last week. It's still the talking point in the bar every night. I still don't know whether to feel embarrassed, sad, amazed or just plain sorry. A bit of them all, I guess.

'It's so daft, I still can't believe it,' admitted the licensee. He took King's proffered tenner and refilled their two modest halves accepting another gold label for himself.

'Old Willie was always in here. He came from the council estate back there,' he said, nodding his head behind him. 'He was always a bit strapped for readies, and most weeks ran up a slate. I didn't mind. Slate runners up always pay up on dole day because they know their tap will be stopped if they don't.

'Well, Willie had half a load on when he arrived and he was on doubles. Anyway, to cut a story short, when I thought he'd had enough I said "That's it Willie", and took him outside to the bus stop. I might have known anything could happen when I saw the bus driver was Big Bernard, who, to say the least, is a bit heavy in the right foot when he gets in that beast. It's been said the dummies in the tailor's window step back when he burns into town.

'I saw Willie onto the bus and the silly sod went upstairs with some difficulty and sat on this side,' he said pointing through the bar window. 'Off goes the bus after another two or three get on and elected to sit downstairs. I was back in here and waved Willie off. He never answered and we all guessed he was past it. Big Bernard got to the estate, unloaded and came back down to town. One of the lads said: "Old Willie's not got off".

'On the next journey the bus stopped outside and I went to the door and waved to Willie and he never bothered to reply. "Miserable bastard," I yelled. After all, he'd been drinking without coughing up. The bus went off again, came back, turned and again stopped outside the pub. But this time a hint of amused interest was creeping in. We were all shouting at him and whistling. He took no notice at all.

'By this time Big Bernard's looking at us as if we're all daft. Down come the bus again, and by now the interest is intense. Of course Willie's seat is on the other side and we can't see up from here whether he's still on it. So we presume he's gone home. The bus completes it's journey and Big Bernard parks it in the garage and knocks off.

'A mechanic drives it through the washer, locks the bus, locks the garage and also knocks off.

'Yeah, you've guessed it. The next morning a new driver picks it up and starts his day, taking some early starters to work. Suddenly a woman lets out an almighty scream. Old Willie's still there.'

'Didn't he say anything?' asked King.

'He was dead,' said Paddy. 'Must have been dead since sinking his last brace of Grouse and me putting him on the bus.'

'So he's one that'll never settle up,' said Jock astutely.

'What about his wife?' asked King.

'She never had a lot of time for him,' said Paddy. 'I thought he'd had a bloody good day out when he came in here.'

'Didn't have such a good night,' said Jock. The three chuckled. 'That's the way to go,' said Paddy. 'Have a healthy – is that the right word – session, run up a slate, pass on in oblivion and be put through the bus wash. I hope it cleansed his soul,' said Paddy crossing himself.

'I hope he kept the window closed and died in his cups rather than the shower,' said King.

16

The boys wandered back into town, still chuckling at the black humour of the story they had just heard.

'That's one you can't use,' said Jock. 'You'd be sued. 'How about some of these famous fish and chips?'

They went to Whitby's famous chippy. 'Good God,' said Jock. 'I've never seen a chippy with waitresses and a wine list before. What do you fancy? It's on me,' he grinned, tapping his top pocket.

'Battered cod, large, and a bottle of beaujolais,' said King, always a man of decision.

Across the pavement the fishing boats were bobbing up and down. The pair polished off their huge meal in the friendly atmosphere. The place was like a North American eatery. Clean tables, no sauce in plastic tomatoes all gungy round the green stalk. There were brasses and things to look at. They felt welcome.

'I once went to one near a cricket ground and you had to fight your way up a flight of steep wooden stairs if you wanted to sit down,' said King.

'There was even a queue on the stairs because the Australians had declared early. Life's changed kiddo.

'And in half an hour it's going to change even more Jock, because we're going back up onto those moors to finish the job. And I've just had an idea.'

'Oh God,' said Jock. 'Spare me Joe. Surprise me. I'm getting used to it.'

On the way to the top the trees in the valley were still bare, spare, sticking up like parsnip roots. Up on the fells the few Christmas trees still had a silvery look from the overnight frost, like those they plant on wedding cakes. The road played hide and seek with the track of the old Pickering steam railway.

'So what's this great idea?' asked Jock. You're beginning to get me nervous again. 'Can't we just fly level for a bit? And by "fly" I mean *'don't'* fly,' he added.

'Look at it this way.' said King. 'All newspapers have what they call morning calls. They check the vicar, the ambulance, the fire service and the police. They ring certain hotels to see if anything untoward has gone on overnight. Common sense, really. We'll get back to a bit of civilisation and make a police call. You just make out you're bright.'

'Like you?' moaned Jock.

'Come on, you soft sod, let's get down the nick, as they say in the trade.'

The village they entered looked po-faced. 'We'll get nothing here Joe,' said Jock.

'Keep your legs together,' grinned King. 'Let's at least give it a go.'

It wasn't exactly what you'd call a police station. There was a council house with a glass box on the wall. 'In case of emergency break glass and use telephone,' said the notice.

'Well, I couldn't really class this as an emergency,' said Jock, as the front window opened and an officer in a blue-ribbed jumper and a police flash on his shoulder looked at them suspiciously. 'Can I help you?' he asked.

'Roving reporters,' said King. 'Sort of coast to coast crime watch.'

'Are you pulling my plonker?' asked the officer who wore gold rimmed spectacles carefully balanced below the bridge of a thin nose.

He didn't look as if he'd got a huge sense of humour. His bike was leaning against the wall with its chain hanging off.

'Seriously,' said King. 'We're doing a cross country of stories. They're different everywhere we've been.'

'Do you drink tea?' asked the officer. 'You look a right pair of buggers to me.'

'Love a cup,' said King. The policeman vanished and in a few seconds the chain on the door dropped with a clunk and they were invited into the office.

There was an old Remington typewriter on the wooden desk, two posters on the wall, one warning of the danger of rabies and the other warning farmers to get their sheep dipped. Ticks, it said, were in season. But the poster was sun bleached and looked as if it had been used as a dart board.

'One lump or two?' asked the constable, whose name it transpired, was Arkwright. 'Now what is it you really want?'

'Seriously,' said King again. 'We're going across the country from west to east and sending stuff over each day. We usually start at the nick,' he lied.

'Burglaries? Drink driving clampdown? Anything unusual up in these here hills?' suggested King.

'Not a great deal,' said PC Arkwright. 'Only rustling.'

'Ah, well it's the time of the season,' said King, almost flippantly. 'You joking?' He realised what he'd said as Jock snorted.

'No, I'm not joking,' said the policeman. 'Big problem, rustling.'

'You make it sound like Okla-bloody-homa,' laughed King.

'It's getting that way,' said the police officer, seriously. 'Go up and see Ted May, the first farm up the valley. He'll tell you how many sheep he's lost this spring. Some of them were even ewes in lamb.

'And the only other incident of note recently was at the rugby club down in Ford. There's this big lorry driver, been a supporter for years, he has. Never any trouble. And they've got this officious steward down there. Now big Mick always liked to finish his half time pint off standing in the clubhouse doorway to see the start of the second half. So there he is doing no harm to anyone when this steward approaches him and apparently says: "I can't let you stand there doing that".

"Doing what?" says Mick.

"Drinking in the doorway", says the steward. He's one of those. 'it's more than my job's worth' types.

'So without further ado big Mick sinks his bitter, picks up the steward in a fireman's lift and carried him to the centre of the field. He drops him in the mud and strides off. The crowd were going mad. You'd think we'd scored at Twickenham. Unfortunately I had to arrest Mick for assault, because the game was being broadcast on Radio White Rose and received huge publicity. I hope he gets off. Court case is next week.'

'Give us his address,' said King. 'Though I don't suppose we can do much with it because it's sub-judice.'

'Correct,' said the policeman. 'But go and see Ted May.'

Outside the pair stood and looked at each other. 'The rugger fan's dead duck,' said King. 'We can't touch that. But what about the rustlers? Let's go and see Farmer May.'

They found the farmstead. It was tucked in the valley side, painted white with the beams recently re-blacked. That was farmer Ted's only pretence to ostentation. The barn and shippons were leaning towards the dilapidated. There were weeds round what had once been a pond. The Land Rover was past its sell-by date. But Farmer May wasn't.

He was a big, taut-chested, strong man. When King and Jock introduced themselves, he swivelled his cap a couple of inches on his broad head, weighed them up and stuck out a hand like a palm tree.

'You'll have got my name from Plod?' They nodded. 'Now this IS a story that needs an end,' said May, wiping a huge hand under a huge nose. 'I'm going to get these bastards. I understand they're coming up here from Pontefract or that area with a cattle truck. They come at the dead of night, sneak into the fields and nick the sheep. I reckon it's cost me two or three grand this winter.'

'Mind if I take down a few details?' asked King. 'We want the facts right. Have they done any other farms?'

'Two in this vale and at least one over the top,' said May. 'Come in and have a glass of rum. Too cold to be standing chopsing out here.'

The farm kitchen still had an old black-leaded range with an oven built-in along side the fire. 'Mabel don't cook in that any more,' he said. There was a modern electric cooker at the far end of the kitchen. 'But it's good for drying my socks in.'

His large features broadened into an amicable grin. 'And I'm going to be out there one night with my twelve bore when those cowboys turn up. And you can print that too. They're messing with the wrong chap.'

Down in the village the pair went walkabout. 'Let's mingle,' suggested King. 'Let's see what this rustling business is about. You go that way, I'll go this. Meet you in the Grapes at midday.'

'High noon,' laughed Jock. 'Keep your head down.'

They went their separate ways, and King gave the office another ring. 'The rustlers' tale stands up,' he told Harris. 'Got facts and figures from a farmer. Just off to see if there's any more been done. It's market day in the next town, and every farmer and his dog's about. I'll file early. I could do it now, but there may be more.'

'Where the hell are you now?' asked Harris, laughing.

King told him, and the news editor was none the wiser.

In the Grapes both reported about 45 minutes early They had drawn a blank, but the barman overheard their conversation, and asked: 'You lads Press?'

'That's right,' said King. 'Understand there's been a deal of sheep stealing recently. How bad is it?'

'It's bad. You want to get over the hill. It's market day. Livestock dealing ends by 2pm. Until then all the lads'll be around. They'll fill you in. But I'd go now.'

The pair finished their halves and scuttled to the next village. They had to park well outside because of rows of cattle trucks, land rovers and cars along the verges. It was still only just after noon as the pals strolled into the town to be met by an amazing sight.

There were a dozen ewes in the ring, but nobody was even looking at them. Farmers, ruddy faced and check-capped were more interested in what was going on outside the ring. There was mighty cheering and shouting and a brawl, like something

152

out of the saloon in old Dodge City was taking place. A police constable was making an unenthusiastic attempt to get through, though what he could have done was the square root of sod all.

The twosome watched the action with some excitement. 'Something's upset that lot,' said Jock, wisely.

King asked a gent in a brown suit and trilby: 'What the hell's going on?'

The gentleman smiled: 'Strangers?'

'We are,' said King.

'Well, it's a little thing called justice. You see those three on the worst end of things? They're getting what they call round these parts, a bloody good pasting. There's been a lot of sheep stealing going on. These three were daft enough to put up some beasts for sale which they'd knocked off. They thought they weren't marked, you see. But Dick Baker, he's the good one with the big right hook, is a smart so-and-so. When all this business rustling began, he didn't put paint marks on his sheep, or brand them, he took a slight clip out of their left ears. Every time strangers came in with sheep to sell he checked for his mark. They came today. See that constable? Well, he'll never get through to break it up. He won't try very hard. Justice can be real rough round here. These three will get the biggest hiding of their lives and will be run out of town. They'll not be back. There'll be no more missing sheep. Nobody'll be any wiser this ever happened. Excuse me. Want to follow them out of town.'

'Nobody'll ever know what happened!' repeated Jock.

'Wanna bet,' grinned King. 'But let's see this through.'

By now the three thieves were deemed to have had enough. As if by instinct the circle around the fight opened and the trio, badly bloodied and bruised, one with a deep bleeding scar on his right cheek, another with a closed eye and the third looking as if he'd just walked out of a motorway argument in a mini against a juggernaught, limped and hopped towards a trailer 100 yards away, the crowd of farmers baying at their heels like hounds on the scent of a vixen.

153

King and Jock followed the melée. Jock, not really understanding the harsh law of the countryside, felt almost sorry for the trio, who scrambled into their vehicle and limped out of town.

'Well, I'm buggered,' said King. 'Did you notice how six or seven of the locals stood in front of the copper so's he couldn't follow and make an arrest or take the trailer's number – even if he'd wanted. They'll not be back. They've had a real sorting.'

'Better than probation, a couple of hundred quid fine or a slap on the wrist from some poofty magistrate who would rather be round at the vicar's for tea and biscuits. It's always been that way in the Lancashire and Cumbrian villages and little towns, Jock. I see it's the same in Yorkshire. They sort things out themselves. But it's still a hell of a story. Let's find a pub with a payphone.'

That didn't take a lot of doing. King got two beers in while he collected his thoughts.

'You've gone quiet, Joe,' said Jock. 'Not funking it are you?'

'Balls,' replied King. 'But this is no daft tale. I have to be careful. The law of the land is involved.'

'It never worried John Wayne.'

'He was usually the sheriff,' laughed King. 'No, I just have to be careful what I tell the desk. Here, shove that phone over will you.'

'Hi Keith,' he said. 'I think I've got a goodie, but we'll have to be careful how it's handled.'

'How does: "Suspected rustlers run out of town after cattle market punch-up:" grab you?'

'Good God Joe, did you *see* this?'

'It was just finishing as I arrived. Three blokes got involved in a hell of a set to because they tried to sell some marked sheep that had gone missing recently. Daft thing to do round here, really. I spoke to a couple of blokes and it appears to be the local custom. If the local farmers see the evidence in front of their eyes and they know where the sheep have come from, they mete out their own justice. I can't use any of the names involved but I've got quotes from another farmer, a bloke called May, who told me the extent of the thieving. I guess these three got off cheaply after what he'd threatened to do to them of he caught them on his land again.'

'And the law. Was there no police presence at this shindig?'

'A local bobby arrived about the same time I did, but he couldn't get near before the three were run out. The copper won't say anything. He'd just get his arse kicked. There's going to be no charges, I'm sure. It's a country matter. The job's been seen to.'

'Let it sing Joe,' said Harris. 'Write it the way you first told me, you know: "Suspected rustlers run out of town after . . . "okay?'

'Give me half an hour, but go through it carefully. Remember, I'm not a professional.'

'Don't worry about that,' laughed Harris, and rang off.

'Well, Jock, I reckon we've earned another pint. I think that one was a bit serious for you and me. We need another daft one.'

'Aye, but there's something in this police-call business,' laughed King. 'We'll try again in the morning.' Jock groaned.

But they didn't have to wait until morning. As King finished filing the sheep tale, a huge figure blocked the light as he filled the doorway. He was wearing plus fours, a plaid shirt and inch-wide braces. 'Say, you guys,' he said. 'Where hell am I?'

The barman, a weedy youth took his life in his hands when he replied: 'We call that the doorway over here.'

The big American looked him up and down coolly as the bar hushed. 'OK, smart-ass. You're one up.' The youth looked relieved and the natives began to chat watchfully again. The card players at the old table under a cracked wall-light in the corner, re-started their game. They were playing three card brag.

The American strolled to the bar and demanded: 'Gimmie a beer buddy. What I guess I meant was to check on which

155

part of England I was in. And before anyone says it, I know it's goddam Yorkshire. You see, I'm looking for an old mate. We were in the Canadian Air Force together. This is his village.' He showed the barman a name on a piece of paper and was told: 'It's about six miles. I'll show you before you go. You alone?'

'Nope. Got my boy with me. Nine he is. From my second marriage.' He strolled to the window to see his child was OK. 'Randall,' he bellowed through the quarter light at the top. 'Stop chasing those goddam pigeons.' And turning to the barman he asked: 'Can he come in here?'

'If he's quiet and doesn't chase things,' said the pimply faced young man. 'What'll he be having?'

'Coke on the rocks. And bring us two chunks of English beefsteak.'

Pimply, who turned out to be called Maurice didn't have the guts to tell him the kitchen had finished cooking. 'I'm sure that can be arranged, sir.'

'Sir? Sir? Jeez, my name's Dan. Don't give me all that Sir crap.'

King said quietly to Jock. 'They could have done with him in the cattle market this morning. He'd have added a bit of spice to this,' he said patting his pocket containing the punch up story he'd just filed.

The American was about 6'5" and around 3' across the shoulders. King's nose started twitching. 'Just come over have you?' he asked the big man.

'Two weeks. Seen it all, done it all. I just wanted to see my old buddy before I go back. He'll be in his sixties now like me. We joined up after the war for the mopping-up jobs. We were over in Italy and western France. Not much to do but fly around. He was the best damned navigator you ever came across. The good lady's still in London packing up and me and the boy came for a last foray. Just six miles away.'

'Want to give him a ring?' offered Maurice. 'Like make sure he's in.'

The American did. 'Hey Orson, how you doin'. Sure it's

Dan. In Arizona? I guess you're half a bubble out of plumb. I'm taking a beer down the road and I'm acomin' to see you in an hour or so. They're going to tell me where your place is. Get some beer in the fridge. See ya pal.'

The American, red-faced and sporting bushy eyebrows, turned to King, who was standing nearby at the bar, looking mildly interested.

'My buddy's real name is Pete. But with a surname like Carte, he's going to be called Orson, isn't he?'

Everyone laughed and the ice was broken. The steaks appeared and were eaten in minutes. The American ordered another beer, asked for a toothpick, of which there were none to hand, and leaned against the bar watching the card players.

They were betting in 10p stakes, double for a blind player. 'That's a kinda cissy way to play,' he said to King. 'Don't they play poker?' King looked at the barman.

Maurice shook his head. 'No they don't they're only the local old boys and the odd out of work youth who play. They keep it that way.'

Big Dan wandered over to the table. 'That's a kinda neat game. Room for another hand?'

The four looked at each other with a certain amount of apprehension. 'OK lads?' one asked the others. 'Okay,' they chorused.

Big Dan sat in, promptly going blind and losing the first four hands. His own first deal came up with a running flush, and two hands later an ace, king, queen against a nine, ten, jack. 'Close, but no cigar,' he grinned at the loser.

King whispered to Jock: 'Have you spotted anything yet?'

Jock replied: 'Only that he's taking all the poor old sods' money.'

'More to it than that,' said King. 'There's a sequence to it. He seems to know when he's got a good hand and stay blind, or when to look and fold them. You don't think he's a conman, do you?'

'Not for a few quid,' said Jock. 'Let's have another half and watch what he's up to.' They watched, but they couldn't spot what was going on. The American by now had a large glass ashtray full of 10p pieces, and the four locals were getting restless, each not wanting to be the first to quit and walk out. Then, to everyone's amazement, the American came clean.

Pushing the cash into the middle of the table, he told them: 'Here you guys. I guess you're not wrapped real tight to play cards for money with a stranger. Fact you're half a bubble out.'

The quartet looked at him dumbly. 'You guys are wondrin' how the hell I did that. I'll show you. It's not cheating. It's not even rememberin'. It's so daft you'll laugh. But you are the privileged four.' He turned his massive back on the rest of the bar and spoke quietly. King watched the players' faces change.

'You see,' said Dan, 'it's down to who spent hands for the last game and in what order he puts them on the bottom of the deck. Once you remember the two best hands and put them in sequence they'll come around next time, sure as clockwork.'

'Bloody 'ell, Alf,' said one of the old boys. 'I wish I'd met this bloke before. It could have changed my life.'

'Remember,' said Dan. 'Don't try to cheat with it or someone will punch you between the eyes. And promise me none of you four will repeat what I have told you to anyone, either in this bar or anywhere else.'

'It's a deal,' said Alf.

'Promise?'

They all nodded.

Dan collected Randall from the dartboard and headed for the exit. 'Always look over your shoulder. Don't let the doorknob hit you where the good Lord split you. And never play with strangers on a train.'

King followed him into the car park and introduced himself. 'You trying to say you can get yourself any hand you want?' he asked.

'Once the sequence comes up. It's the same at poker.'

'What's your surname? I'd love to do a piece for my paper about the day the Yank hit town and showed the locals a clean pair of heels.'

158

'Sure buddy, I don't mind that. The name's Branton. We gotten an antique shop in Prescott, just down from Whiskey Row. That's partly why I'm over here, looking for old stuff to ship home. Here's my card. Send me a copy. That'll get them blinking in the bars back home. It's only a schoolboy trick really. It's the presentation that matters,' he winked, crushed the wincing King's hand, and said: 'Now, where's this motherin' village?' King had listened to Maurice's instructions, and pointed. He went back into the bar where Jock was laughing, watching the four card players trying out their new route to untold wealth.

'They've forgotten it already I reckon,' said the Scot. 'They're larger than life some of these Yanks. Give 'em that.'

'And give me that phone,' said King. 'I've got to tell Harris about this one. Keith? Joe here. Think I've got another goodie. How's about a giant Yank who came into a moorland market village and showed the locals how to deal themselves any hand at brag?'

'For God's sake Joe, I can't keep up with you. We're still talking to the lawyer about the cattle market business. Oh! It's OK. I've just had the thumbs up from the editor. Knock your card sharp stuff over first thing in the morning and take a day off. Well done.'

King turned to his mate. 'Jock, I'm about knackered. Let's go back to the van. I just want to put my feet up and have a cup of tea for once. And you can make us one of those bacon butties.

'We've got the day off tomorrow. We'll just make that police call and then you can go and paddle in the icy briny if you want. Let's go.'

17

The chain had still not been fixed on the bobby's bike. When he came to the door he still wore his glasses like an old lady balancing a pair of pince nez on a narrow, chapel nose. The only difference King noticed was that the blue lamp over the door was switched on.

'You two again,' muttered P.C. Arkwright. 'Any luck with the rustlers?'

'Well it wasn't exactly Rawhide, but it turned out to be interesting. It's 'sort it out yourself' country this, isn't it?' He didn't want to drop other lawman in it for not entering the foray and making an arrest.

'I understand it was sorted out,' said the blue-jumpered policeman, who was now wearing his sergeant's flashes, the chevrons on his arm like adverts for petrol. He had put on the Velcro stickers in a hurry at hearing the doorbell. They were not quite in line, like his specs.

'Your blue lamp is still on,' said Jock. 'It makes me feel like Jack Warner.'

'He was shot by Dirk Bogarde,' sniffed the sergeant. 'Now, what can I do for you today? No time for tea, I've a court case in Whitby. No rustlers today. No fights. No burglaries. No suspicious deaths. All I can offer is a local MP's son stopped on a motorcycle at 1am today.'

'Pissed?' asked King, directly.

'Breathalyser clear as that stream,' said the sergeant. 'But it looked a wee bit funny at first. He was wearing nothing but pyjama trousers and a top hat.'

'As you do,' said Jock. 'Come on Serge, what's all this

160

about? What was he doing, going home from a fancy dress party?'

The sergeant removed his spectacles, wiped his eyes, and laughed. 'Go out and ask him. He's a silly bugger, that's for sure. But he was stone cold sober. And probably freezing his balls off.'

'What's his name?' asked King. 'And where do we find him?'

'Name's Willie Webber. Father's also William, Conservative MP for this constituency. Willie's in antiques in a big way. His humour still exceeds his business acumen. His emporium's in Scarborough, but he's usually on the road.'

'In jim-jams and a top hat?' King couldn't help asking the question.

'Big business,' said the sergeant. 'The lad's worth a fortune. Only 24. Not married. Not got all the devilment out of him yet. Lives at the family pile, Willington Grange. Father spends most of his time in London, of course, so our wee Willie can get away with just about what he likes. But Mother Webber is a bit of an old stickler.

'Try the Grange about 6pm. He may be back – or in the Wheel, where I understand he stops off for one on the way home,' said the policeman, tapping his nose as if he knew the inns and outs of all his locals. He uses the Wheel and he's still got a schoolboy sense of fun. A joker – so watch your backs if you go to find him. But I'm sure he'll tell you about the top hat incident. It'll need a bit of delicate treatment by you two, though.

'You'll find the Grange between here and the coast. Long track up to the right. Silly so and so would have frozen to death pulling a stunt like that a month ago. Good job it's getting warmer. See you lads.'

'Getting warmer!' grunted Jock. 'God, they're like polar bears up here. We going to see him?'

'Course we are,' said King. 'Six o'clock sharp. Now let's go and have another look at Whitby. I want to get Maggie some of that jet and the kids a couple of boxes of that local fudge.'

'Given up on the rock?' asked Jock, getting a knowing look from his mate.

The trees were coming into bud and the weeds threatening to surge into their April sprint. The east wind had retreated to Siberia. It was degrees milder.

In Whitby harbour the moored fishing boats, tied together, were nudging each other like interested elderly trippers with something to point out. Young mothers were comparing babies in their prams. The kids were warm and muffled and couldn't give a stuff that the woman in the red hat thought they looked just like their cousin Betty. The mothers were smiling benignly, fishing for compliments, all the time believing their offspring was a far superior specimen.

Two fishing smacks were racing each other for the harbour jaws, both pushing white moustaches of foam at their noses.

'I guess last in pays for the beer,' said King, watching the boats and the gulls soaring expectantly.

'Good idea,' said Jock, steering his chum on a course to the door of the pub they were passing. The sea had gone flat. The public bar was making do with two glowing strands of electric fire, stuffed into the fireplace instead of the coal and logs.

'Spring must be in the air,' muttered Jock. 'How about a pint and fish and chips again?'

'Your turn for the house red,' said King. 'We'll have to take it easy though. We've got to go back into the hills for six o'clock. I wonder just what his lordship was up to.'

'I can't wait to find out,' said Jock.

The entrance to Willington Grange was imposing. The wrought iron gates were anchored back and the stone pillars on each side, acting as upper class gate posts, were mounted by two huge stone balls.

'That's what this could end up as Jock, a load of balls,' grinned King.

'Have faith, my trusty friend,' said the Scot. 'If this turns out to be a winner we'll have only one more stunner to find before we return to sanity and our loved ones.'

'Aye, that's if they're still there. Maggie was getting a bit uptight last night. If my stuff wasn't getting in the Press she'd think I was shacked up with some bird in Windermere.'

'You nearly were,' quipped his mate.

'That was Ambleside,' said King, a bit testily, knowing how near his mate was to the truth.

The drive to the hall was about half a mile long, with a bracken moor on the left and pine woods to the right. They swept round a bend and saw the splendid early Georgian house. There were impressive stone pillars framing the strong, oak front door. The windows were leaded, the gardens neat, and a small front lawn was separated from the house by a grand drive. The lawn sported – or boasted – more stone in the form of a stylish sundial.

'Fond of their stone,' said King as he scrunched to a halt on the loose shingle. 'I hope to God our Willie's in after all this.'

To the right of the house was a fast running stream which looked like an out of work mill-race. It brushed shoulders with the old building where it met a solid buttress, and then stepped aside like a lively rugby three-quarter, bubbling over the boulders.

'How the other half live,' grinned King, ringing the bell. It was some time before they heard any movement. Then the door opened and a small man in his fifties opened the door and inspected them.

'Er, Mr Webber?' asked King, knowing full well it wasn't. And he didn't know whether to call the MP Sir anyway, had it been him.

'I'm Clifford,' he said, adding without noticeable humour: 'Odd jobs and garden. Begonias a speciality.'

'Is Mr Webber in?' asked King.

'Junior or Senior?' asked Henry Clifford.

'Junior,' said King.

'He is still at business. We never know quite when to expect him home. Could be any time, Mr William Senior is in the House.'

'Well, could I have a word with him?' asked King.

'The House of Commons,' sniffed Clifford, rather too grandly.

'Mrs Webber in?' asked King, his rising dander making him feel more determined.

'She doesn't like to be disturbed at this time of day,' intoned the servant. 'But I'll ask her. Who shall I say is calling and what shall I say it's about?'

'It's a Press enquiry,' said King, who had by now decided he was not to be put off having got so far. 'It's nothing serious. I'm Joe King from the Evening Press. Just a bit of a local story, that's all.'

Clifford looked at him askance and went indoors, not asking them in. 'I remember that as a kid,' said King. 'You'd go round on your bike to see if someone was coming out to play football, and their mothers used to leave you on the cold sodding step. As if they'd something to hide. Yet at our house all the other kids used to come round to get changed and have hot chocolate. Funny old world.'

In some two minutes a small, scrawny woman appeared. She was dressed for dinner in an expensive looking outfit and had a rope of pearls like white marbles round her neck.

'Yes?' she said briskly.

'I'm King of the Evening Press,' said the intrepid reporter, immediately realising that sounded worse than saying he was Joe King. 'And this is my friend and assistant Henderson. It was your son we really wanted a word with. Nothing serious. Just something about a motorbike.'

'I don't think he's got one of those,' said Mrs Webber. 'He deals more in William and Mary furniture. And silver, of course. He could be back any time, but he said he won't be dining here this evening. But call again, if it's really necessary. Good night to you,' she said, closing the heavy door like a bank safe.

'So it's got to be the Wheel,' grinned Jock. 'This evening would seem to have a wee bit of promise.'

'Spot on,' said King, laughing at his mate's sudden enthusiasm. 'Let's go and find it. I saw a sign on the way from the Whitby chippy.'

164

A crack of a full moon was peeping through the dark clouds as the camper retraced its journey. 'A bombers' moon,' said Jock seriously, temporarily startling King who was mentally working out his plan of attack.

'You what?' he said.

'A bombers' moon,' repeated Jock, knowingly. 'They used to call it that in the war. There was light enough to know where they were but cover the ME 109s darted in. And then our Spits and Hurricanes could nip in and out of the cloud to harry and dodge the Kraut fighters.'

'How do you know all this?' asked King, again seriously. 'Look out Skip, this is the turn for the Wheel.'

'You should have been a bloody navigator,' laughed King, still glad of his daft mate's company. His sarcasm was well-meaning.

The Wheel was tucked off the main road in what was now a lay-by left by road straightening. It was an odd sort of place. The lounge and restaurant to the right of the front door was a partial refurb: more an extension of the pub.

Its walls were adorned with carefully made reproductions of old shop signs – even to the cracks in the varnish. Old looking farm implements, that had never seen a field, were suspended from the ceiling. It was empty.

But the bar to the left was real. It was full. It had a bare floor, but no affectation of sawdust. It had a nine-pin skittle board with ball and chain. It was as happy as the lounge was yuppie. Tourists would use the other bar and ask for pub grub menus. The real bar was down to pints and whiskies.

'This'll do for me,' said Jock, ordering two pints. The couple checked around them. They didn't even know what Willie Webber looked like. They got a cheery welcome from behind the bar from a well-built youth who looked as if he'd come by tractor. The locals nodded and King and Jock stood back watching the vivial bunch at play.

A young fellow in a grey lounge suit, no pin stripes, said to a friend at the end of the bar: 'Try one for the ditch Willie?'

Jock looked at his mate, who had already clocked the

165

comment, and winced. 'Here we go again. Pound to a piece of something rude that's our man.'

'Owd thee foot up,' said King, turning his Lancashire accent up a notch. 'Not so fast. Let's watch a while.'

He went to the bar and purposely stood by the number one target. Ordering two cheese and pickle sandwiches he turned to his suspect like a modern Sherlock, and enquired: 'You're not Willie Webber by any chance?'

'Certainly am,' said the young man amiably, taking a quaff out of a pint of bitter. 'And how can I be of help to you sir?'

Webber was wearing an expensive tweed sports jacket, cavalry twill slacks and his brogues were as well-polished as his face which reflected a healthy life on the east coast. He wasn't over tall, but solidly proportioned. He looked as if he's be useful in a rugger scrum. He had twinkling eyes under a head of brown curly hair that was beginning to thin.

He was drinking with a tall, thin man, perhaps a couple of years older. His suit had seen perhaps more town than country. Both men looked as if they had been laughing and were smoking small, thin cigars with their beer. Both looked at King with question marks on their faces.

'If you could spare me a couple of minutes I'd be grateful. I'm a reporter from the west coast. This is my chum Jock. We're doing a coast to coast pub crawl in search of daft stories.'

'Jeez, you sound a man after my own heart,' laughed Webber. 'If you're on expenses we'll have another pint.'

King obliged and the two locals led the way to a corner table. Webber introduced his pal as one Dickie Delamere. 'Watch him, he's crackers,' he joked.

'Is it about the antiques road show?' Webber asked.

'Not exactly,' said King. 'It's about being caught on a motor bike in the middle of the night wearing little more than a top hat.'

Webber looked at him, initially seriously and then his face broke into a grin. 'How the hell did you hear of that?' he asked, with public school cadences.

'Know the local sergeant,' said King. 'Regular sense of humour he has!'

'Well,' said Webber. 'Fancy the boys in the marmalade sandwich reporting that. Can this be a police state I ask myself? And I hadn't had a drop.' He was laughing from his stomach, wobbling silently.

His mate Delamere was a little more raucous and was chortling loudly.

'So what happened to the local MP's son to find himself in such a fix?' laughed King, infected by the lightheartedness the incident had been greeted with. The landowner's son and his mate were obviously not at all worried, as you often find in silly situations with the upper crust of society. On a council estate the two reporters would by now have been advised to leave or risk a punch in the face for daring to pose such personal questions. King decided, rather quickly, he could have backed another winner, and decided to take it gently.

'Big in antiques, aren't you Willie?' asked King, carefully.

'Biggest in the north east,' said Webber. 'Our main base is Scarborough, but we have branches right up to Newcastle and inland to the market towns. It's a good old family business. Dad turned the running of it over to me when his hand was raised by the returning officer at the last election.

'All you have to remember is not to get greedy. There's enough for everyone. We give fair prices and free valuations. We sell right, taking only a legal 10 per cent. I hope you're going to get some of this in your daft piece.' He laughed again.

'It fits like a sock,' said King, wondering how he was gong to do it. He was not in the business of advertising blurbs. 'Now tell me about the motorbike incident.'

Webber looked at him shrewdly. King knew he was not dealing with someone who had just fallen off the turnip truck. 'It was so daft I still can't believe it. And I hadn't had a drink all night, honest. I'd been to a fair at Harrogate.

'It was mother's bridge night and she'd turned in as soon as her friends left. She's a bit of a miserable old sod. Not exactly full of bonhomie. Luckily I'm told I take after the old man. Well, mother doesn't sleep well and takes a Micky Finn or something. When I got home everyone was in bed. So for once in my life I made a coffee and went up to bed to read a catalogue I'd picked up in Harrogate. Suddenly all hell was let loose. There was the roar of a big motor cycle which came up the drive as if Agostini was winding it back. Sprayed gravel all over the place. Almost broke the lounge window by the sound of it. My bedroom is at the front. Luckily mother's is at the back.

'I opened my window, there's Tricky Dickie here sitting on this damn great machine shouting: "Got a minute old boy? Something to show you".

'"Sod off", I told him. "If you wake mother we'll both get an earful. You know what she's like".'

His chum Dickie took up the story: 'Pity old Webber has such a tight-arse mother,' he laughed, looking at his pal for confirmation and taking another swig.

'Dead right,' agreed Webber. 'She doesn't seem to see the funny side of things. Different again from the old man. He can be a rare joker. Pulled some real stunts in his time.'

'Spot on old thing,' laughed Dickie. 'Now he's kidding half the country from Westminster.' The pair, obviously close pals, continued their banter. 'Come on Dellers,' said Willie. 'Talk to the Press.'

'Right,' said Dickie. 'It was like this. And I still don't believe it myself. I'd invested in a new Kawasaki. Big job. Seven fifty cc. Anyway I'd had a couple of pints on the way home from work and after dinner. I was reading through the handbook and decided to go for a quick spin to try her out. Dead sober I was, honest. I guess it was around midnight. Thought I'd pop round and show Willie what I'd bought.

'You can't beat the feel of screaming around the countryside on two wheels. The old wind in your face. It wasn't even a cold night. So I had a spin round the lanes and nipped up to the Grange. Willie's light was still on, so I gave her a couple of rev ups. With alarming speed he opened the window. I thought he was bollock naked. It was only when I took my visor off he realised it was me.

'"Bugger off", he said. "You'll wake the old girl". So I

gave her another couple of revs, know what I mean? And he came down to the front door, trying to shoo me off as if I was a randy donkey.

'"Just something to show you Willie", I told him. He was not at all polite.

'"Just get on the back and we'll go up the drive", I said. All he was wearing was his jim jam trousers. Silk too . . . Not even his slippers. To get rid of me he sat on the back of the bike and I opened her up. Shingle flying everywhere. As I got near to the gate I realised I had got the old sod over a barrel, so to speak. Now it was his turn. One back for locking me on the stage with the police choir as they were singing On The Road to Manderlay.'

'You what?' enquired King, no longer surprised at anything. He looked at Webber who was laughing into his pint. 'Come on, let's have it!'

'We went into Scarborough to play in a snooker tournament at the Conservative club. Seeing he was familiar with the club I believed him when we left the side bar of the Rabbit and nipped through a back alley. He said if we went up the back stairs and through the fire door it would save us waiting all round the front . . . It was, he said, the easiest way to the snooker room. He even opened the door for me and ushered me in.

'The baritone was just on the 'Where the flying fishes play' bit as I heard the door snap shut behind me. I tried the release bar, but he was holding the door from the top step outside.

'Half the bloody choir faltered and turned to look at me. There was a rustle of amazement from the audience. The blue rinse brigade and the big hats were out in force. The pianist played on and I had to stand there with the choir, pretending I was in the choir, until they had finished. Then I left the stage, nodding with acute embarrassment through the audience to the bar across the corridor opposite. There he was, hanging onto the bar unable to speak, apoplectic with laughter. I told him: "I'll get you for that you red faced bastard". Now I reckon it's one a piece.

'I was waiting my chance . . . So there we were doing about

sixty along this lane. Poor old Willie was getting a bit chilly on the pillion, knocking me on the back to turn round. Oh no! I could only see that police choir. Then I spotted something on the road and pulled up. Willie was bellowing something about pneumonia when I realised the object was a top hat, obviously thrown out of a car by some celebrating wedding party. I picked it up and told him to put it on if he was cold.

'I decided I wanted a leak and not risking leaving the engine running and getting marooned, I took out the key and nipped through a farm gate to relieve myself. They say you can never find a policeman when you want one. Oh, dearie, dear! There I am behind the hedge when round the corner comes this jam sandwich. Obviously it pulled up and out steps one officer, looking in amazement at the apparition sitting on the bike. Silk pyjamas and nothing else but a top hat. Well, what's he going to think?

'Naturally I kept mum in the field, trying not to laugh too loudly as he tried to answer the questions. He actually said he was being shown a new bike. The officer looked around him and said: "In a top hat and pyjamas Sir? And who exactly is showing you this machine?"

'Willie tried to explain that the owner of the bike had run out of petrol, searching desperately for the fuel-off tap. Well, it got more and more confused. The officer wanted to know about crash helmets, and why the owner had taken off across the fields to the farm to get some petrol.

'But he's a jammy so and so. It turned out the copper knew his dad. He just said: "I daren't ask any more Willie. Just whistle up your mate, wherever he is and get back to bed. Not been drinking by any chance have we?"

'"Not a drop Pete, honest", said Willie. "Give me the machine and I'll blow for as long as you like. I'm not even driving".

'The squad car drove into the night. Bet they're still talking about it in the mess at the nick. Must have been the biggest mystery they've come across for years.'

Willie, who had obviously enjoyed the re-telling of the tale as his expense, grinned: 'The tables will be turned. Vengeance is sweet. I don't know how the hell he did it. One minute I'm lying in bed reading, all warm and at peace, the next I'm being stopped by the police astride the back of a bloody great motorbike wearing a top hat and no tails. Jeez.

'Sure you can use it in your paper. But make it light-hearted. Mention the old man and don't make me sound too daft. Though I guess I am and always will be,' laughed Willie. 'I'll tell you one thing, I will get some stick at the rugger club's annual thrash. Peter the copper is a member. I guess that's why I'm not in Broadmoor. Even so, his mate pointed that breathalyser at me like a pistol. It was when I said "Don't shoot, I'll come quietly", that they just looked at me and drove off. I raised my hat to them. I'll get this bastard Dickie back for that one.'

The two shook hands over the table and laughed warmly together. It was a lovely atmosphere. The air was thick with fun. 'I'm going to ring Maggie,' said King.

As he eased himself from the bench behind the worn wooden table, the back door of the bar which led to the gents and the cigarette machine, burst open. A huge figure wearing wide, red braces over the yellow plaid shirt, stormed in, filling the doorway as he took in the scene. His eyes fell on the four at the table.

'Well kiss a fat man's ass,' he exclaimed.

'God, it's Desperate Dan again,' exclaimed Jock. 'Wonder if he found his mate.'

'He did,' said Willie. 'And he bought £2,000 worth of antiques off me this morning. 'See, as I said, give 'em a fair crack and they'll buy the goods.'

'Fancy you four being buddies,' said Dan, approaching their table. 'Bought some great gear from Mister Webber here this morning for shipping home. Rounded off my trip a treat.

'Say, I didn't know you guys were in here. I've been trying some local cod and fries in the other bar. Staying with old Pete again tonight. Right now he's playing some damned soft board game with young Randall. I wanted a last look at a Yorkshire pub. Jeez, it's as cold as a well-digger's lunch bucket out there.'

171

'It is if you're in pyjamas and a top hat,' laughed Dickie.

'How's that?' said the giant American.

'Local joke,' said Webber hurriedly, trying desperately to keep up his front as an international antiques dealer.

'Well, I got to leave you assholes. If you're ever States-side, anywhere near Prescott, you've got my card. Even if you're visiting Yellowstone or the Grand Canyon, gimme a ring. We'll go to the bars on Whiskey Row, shoot some pool, drink a few beers and throw up. All the normal shit.' With that he threw a fiver on the bar and said: 'Give these guys a beer.' And he was gone.

'Sort of larger than life, aren't they?' said Webber. 'But I don't think he's caught up with the price of English pints yet.'

'A bit boisterous,' smiled King, completing his interrupted journey to the door to find the phone.

'When are you back Joe?' asked Maggie, sounding fed up. 'The kids need a firm hand. I'm missing you love. I know you've had some fun and I reckon you're famous back here. The Press has done a piece about circulation figures. They're more than a thousand up on the ABC figures last year, it says. One of the reasons they give is your little adventures which seem to have caught the imagination locally.

'I just hope to God they don't offer you a job. Can't you get an ice cream cart or something? The spring flowers are all coming through on the prom now.'

'Too seasonal,' laughed King. 'It'll be about two days now and I'll be home. One more pub and then the ceremony of reaching Robin Hood's Bay. We'll be sober, don't worry. It's a long trip home.

'Love you,' said King and rang off before the call got maudlin. Back in the bar Jock had subsidised big Dan's fiver and bought a round. 'I paid the difference,' explained the Scotsman.

'God, Carnegie had nowt on you Jock,' said King. 'How you fixed for donating a library or two?' They finished their beer and said their goodbyes to Willie and Dickie.

'I hope to hell I've done the right thing,' said Webber,

suddenly looking as if he may have second thoughts. 'Make it a fun piece Joe. Nothing serious or they'll have me put away.'

'And then mater would evict him,' grinned Dickie cheekily.

18

Each day was getting warmer as the sun rose and lost its watery eye of winter. 'One more pub and I think that's it,' said King. His pal heaved a sigh of relief. 'And where's it going to be? You've not heard something have you?' he asked nervously.

'There's one. Dickie told me about it last night as we were leaving the Wheel. It's got a ghost.'

'That's all we need,' replied Jock. 'We've had the invisible man. Now a headless boozer in the public bar will about complete the set. Where is it?'

'I reckon that is it,' said King, pulling off the bumpy road on their back route to the coast. 'See through there Jock. That could be it. I know it's in sight of the sea.'

The inn looked nothing much. Tucked away in a little hamlet in a quiet valley which led down to the north sea. It was stone-built and tiny with bare, bony fingers of winter trees clasping at its tiled roof. 'The village where time stood still,' breathed Jock.

The pair went into the one and only bar to be met by a cheerful, rosy-faced woman in her late thirties – or so they guessed. The window was small and the light over the optics was of low wattage. 'They don't give owt away in Yorkshire,' whispered King under his breath. Jock heard him and smiled. The female behind the bar obviously did not.

Jock ordered two halves seeing it was only 10.30am. 'Want your tie cut off?' the well-fed female asked him.

'You what?' said Jock, taken aback. He had put on his Scottish golf club's tie so to arrive at their coastal destination looking smart, as if hoping the cameras would be awaiting them.

'I'm Joan,' said the smiling black-haired landlady. She was wearing slacks which accentuated her curves and a shirt of bright colours. She reached under the bar and produced a pair of scissors.

'If you don't have your tie cut off you have to tell me a poem.'

'You what?' repeated Jock, leaving King stomaching his laughter whilst standing back watching the action. He had a huge, expectant grin across his broad face.

'Look,' said Joan, pointing to the beams around the bar. The bottom halves of hundreds of club ties which had been snipped off their owners and pinned to the woodwork.

'You can't have this one,' said Jock, covering the crossed clubs on his blue tie with a protective hand. 'It's the only one I've got, and I never get back up there these days to get another. May we please have our lagers.'

'No tie, then give me a poem for my anthology,' said Joan firmly, pushing the glasses towards him and snipping the scissors threateningly.

'Er. There was a young man from Dundee, Whose . . .'

'Know it,' said Joan.

'There was a big tart from South Hants . . .'

'Know it.'

'Well. It was midnight in Market Street, Manchester . . .'

'Dirty sod, know it,' said Joan, triumphantly.

'God, what's all this about. Am I on Candid Camera?' stuttered Jock.

King could no longer contain himself and wheezed at his friend's embarrassment. 'Keep going Jock,' he chortled.

'I eat my peas with honey.

'I've done it all my life.

'I know it might sound funny,

'But it sticks them to the knife,' said Jock weakly. It was all he could think of, by now being thoroughly confused.

'That's got you off the hook,' said Joan. 'But it's not very good, is it? Say it again and I'll write it down. You may think I'm barmy, but it's all in a good cause.

175

'A local printer who comes in here has agreed to knock off a few hundred copies of my anthology and we're selling it for the kids' charity. It'll go towards the bunce from the summer fete fund. The lads in the darts and dominoes teams are running it all. They look after the kitty. I get 25p for a ditty and 50p for a tie at local functions. A lot of it goes towards Mencap.'

Jock heard King hooting like a choking owl behind him. 'I'm not surprised,' he said, rather unkindly.

It was only then that King noticed there was another figure in the bar, a slightly built, darkly-dressed man sitting quietly in a dark recess to the side of the stone fireplace.

He nudged Jock and indicated with a nod towards the figure. Jock started. He'd had enough for one morning.

Joan noticed their glances and laughed. 'Oh, don't worry about him. That's Hissing Sid. Reckons he's seen Clara more than anyone else.'

'Clara?' asked King, realised he was now getting some of the treatment himself. 'Who the hell's Clara?'

'Our resident ghost. Hissing Sid comes in twice a day and claims to have seen Clara eight times over the years. Never talks much, just watches.'

'Why do they call him Hissing Sid?' asked Jock, obviously.

'Well, he developed this hiss when he had his teeth out. Became conscious of it and hardly talks at all now,' Sid could obviously hear everything that was being said in the small bar, but took no notice.

King walked towards him and said: 'Morning Sid, may I get you a drink?'

'Eight,' said Sid.

'You what?' said King startled.

'Schee Clara eight timsh.'

King bought him a Guinness and said: 'Who is Clara, Sid?'

'Schee wash killed by the mad parschon. Comesh out of that wall and vanisches there,' he said pointing to the opposite side of the bar. He would say no more, and King returned to the servery.

'Look Joan,' he said. 'We're reporters from the Evening

Press. Is there anything in this? A bit of publicity might help your Mencap appeal.'

'Folk lore, I reckon,' said the landlady. 'Never seen Clara myself. But we had a barmaid who did and she left the same night. Old Clara has a mention in some history book if you can be bothered to go to Whitby reference library. Personally I think it's just a good story.'

'What's Sid's surname? Do you think he'd mind a mention in the paper?'

'I don't even think he'd notice it,' said Joan, looking at the small, skinny figure in the corner. 'Not much of him, is there? Wouldn't think he drank all that Guinness. His name's Gee.'

'Bet he never gets mouthy,' laughed Jock. 'There you are Joe, tie snipping, poem telling and a ghost all in one morning.'

After more banter with Joan the duo left for the coast. King stopped to ring Harris and tell him of their final tale.

'I thought you were on you way home Joe?' said the news editor. 'I think you've done more than enough.'

'Just one more,' said King. 'Then we've got to dip our feet in the north sea. Traditional, you know. I'll file the ghost and the ties and the odd odes from Robin Hood's Bay and ring you in the morning.'

'Well done, mate,' said Harris. 'You still married?'

'Just,' said King. 'See you.'

The last night was spent cleaning up the van. 'We'll have to put it through the wash before we return it,' said King. 'But it's done us proud. We'd never have got on this without it.'

'I wonder what happened to the office car,' twinkled King. 'That must be driving them mad. It'll teach the bastards to treat their reps right. So sod 'em.'

As they'd not done much cooking and only the necessary washing of clothes, the camper didn't need much treatment.

Forgetting it was Saturday, and Harris was taking his day off, King filed anyway. 'Still out with the pick and shovel doing a bit of trenching, Joe?' laughed the copytaker, who was in to take stuff for early pages on Monday and cover the afternoon's sport.

'Not long now, love,' said King. 'Last day, I reckon.'

'I'll bet you two buggers have had some fun,' she said. 'I've had Keith Harris standing in here asking if you'd been on and what you'd turned up next.'

'Well, sweetheart, I reckon that's about it. I'll bring you lasses a big box of chocolates to gorge next week. Or would you prefer a bottle of sherry?'

'Guess,' said cheeky Lisa. 'Come and have one with us.'

They reached Robin Hood's Bay. They were high above the village. In the summer no cars are allowed down the steep hill between the souvenir shops, the hotel, the antique shop and the summer rentals. In March, even late March, you should be able to drive down. But there was the dreaded yellow 'Road closed for repairs,' sign at the top, so they had to use the summer tourists' car park and walk down to the harbour.

Kings Brook gurgled in playfully from the right and the wind still had a bit of a knife in it as it snook in from the sea to the east.

There were a couple of battered and useless old fishing boats by the slipway and King looked cautiously at the grey ocean.

'Right, chum, this is it. Dip your feet in the North Sea. Follow me.' He sat on the wall, discarded his shoes and socks and walked down the shingle.

After 10 yards he turned to see Jock hadn't moved. 'Come on you soft bugger,' he said.

'But I only joined your cross country half way.'

'Then just put one foot in,' laughed King. 'Either that or I leave you here.'

King clenched his teeth as the ripples crossed his lily-white feet. 'God that's straight from the Arctic,' he grimaced, leaving the water quickly, pleased with himself that he'd done it.

He watched Jock, who had had to remove both shoes and socks so as not to get the non-participant left wet and salty-white. Jock saw a ripple coming, dipped his right foot in, murmured 'Jesus Christ' and scampered up the beach to find the warmth of his thermal socks and walking shoes.

'Come on you big soft sod,' said King. 'Let's get this show on the road. Wagons-west!'

'No more pink rock?' asked Jock. 'Get them another lump and your pair will have enough to start their own quarry.'

'Not a bad idea,' said King, seriously. He went into the rock shop nearest the beach and bought another couple of sticks. Then they puffed up the hill. 'God, this trip has done me no good at all,' groaned Jock. 'I came for a break and I feel like a rugby ball.'

'Get in man,' said King as they reached the camper. 'One more stop.'

'Hell fire, I thought that was it,' moaned the Scot.

'What day is it?' asked King, rhetorically.

'Saturday.'

'And what happened on a Saturday?'

'Oh no, not that bloody Saturday Club? Where was it now?'

'Pull yourself together lad,' said King. 'Just through Richmond. It's not that far. Do you regret any of this Jock?' asked King, being serious. 'You've long been AWOL after your 48 hour pass. You in trouble?'

'Away man,' said Jock, also seriously. 'Like your Maggie, she knew I needed a break. We didn't have the best of times at Cunliffe's did we? Every time I ring the lassie tells me just to get it out of my system. I reckon we're lucky with our women, Joe.'

The caravette threaded its way through Richmond and back into the open country.

'Wonder what they're up to at the Rhubarb and Custard this morning,' said Jock.

'We'll soon find out. There it is.'

'Do you believe all that's gone on since we were last here?' Jock asked his mate. 'It's too silly to think about.'

Their timing was perfect. The couple strolled into the public bar and there was Annie doing a card trick at the bar. Pith helmet and flying goggles were captivated. She looked up as the pair entered.

'Good God, look what's turned up,' she laughed.

'Greenhouse Joe and his Scottish chum. How'd you get on lads?'

Before they could answer she gave them both a peck on the cheek and a pint of lager – which King insisted on paying for. 'Know any card tricks?' she asked.

'No, but I know a Yank who can deal himself any hand he wants at three card brag.'

'Where is he?' asked Annie, her face lighting up. 'We could use him in the crib team.'

'Gone back to Arizona,' said King. 'He thought everyone round here was barmy.'

'Not far out, was he?' laughed the vivacious Annie, completing her trick, which nobody seemed to understand.

'No footballers or fire eaters today?' enquired Jock.

'Now there's a thing,' said the landlady. 'Ray's playing, of course, but Pedro's in hospital.'

'What, heartburn?' quipped King.

'Not exactly. He sucked when he should have blown and singed his lungs, or something. He's said to be "comfortable". But it doesn't sound too cosy to me. There he was, doing his trick when he lets out a terrible gurgle. We had to force a half of chilled lager down his throat before calling the quack. He's OK. He'll be out today. God willing . . .'

'Here we go again,' offered Jock. 'Can't we go home? Please.'

'Jock lad, you signed on for a couple of days and have done a couple of weeks or so. You're not quitting now.' King said to Annie: 'No marbles today, or knife throwing or magic rope tricks. Hell, what a quiet Saturday for the Rhubarb and Custard.'

The landlady laughed: 'Don't hold your breath. It doesn't start on the bell, it sort of evolves.' And glancing at the door, she laughed: 'Look who's here!'

The lads turned. Entering the scene was Floyd – minus Gladys.

'Not brought the missus today?' smiled Pith Helmet.

'It's take time for a couple of months, then it's give and take for a couple of Saturdays. Have you ever thought how much room women take up in pubs?'

'She doesn't mind because she's a bit slow on the uptake. She thinks high dudgeon is a Lakeland fell. But she had me this morning, she told me I was like a weekend cottage, only in two days a week and the rest of the time vacant. She comes from Wales you know. Do you know, she saw me doing my exercises this morning and told me I looked like an earnest karate enthusiast from Barnoldswick.'

By now everyone was laughing. Flying Helmet and Goggles ordered another pint and when Annie reached out for his fiver it shot back into his pocket at the speed of light.

'Bloody hell,' she said.

'It's me little trick,' he said. 'It's me item of interest for this week.'

'Come on sunshine,' demanded Annie. 'Let's have a look at it.'

'Should be ashamed of yourself, big lass like thee,' said the cheery, beery face under the leather headgear. 'Here you are. Bought it on Whitby front. It's me whizzer. See, it's on this thin nylon and when you release the button it whizzes back to you.' He let it go again to the amazement of the gathering. 'Gladys said she wasn't surprised I have to come out for a drink at dinner because I'm a professional snorer. Gives me a thirst, you know.'

The ribbing went on and King slipped out back to phone Maggie. 'Home tonight pet. Just stopped off for a bit of lunch.'

'Sounds a nice quiet pub you've found,' she said pointedly as a fresh wave of laughter crackled into the passage.

'Aye, they tend to be a bit raucous at weekend up here.'

'You're not in that Saturday club thing are you?'

King kept forgetting his experiences had been shared through the power of the Press.

'I'll be back mid-evening love. Don't worry, we're OK. We're sober and are going to stay that way. It's a tidy drive.'

Back in the raunchy bar, Floyd was still at it. 'Do you know I haven't done anything I regretted for years. There must be something wrong with a bloke who has to admit that.'

'Go and ping a pellet through that greenhouse next door,'

grinned Jock. 'That'll be twelve quids worth of regret.'

The banter carried on into the early afternoon, King not drinking because of driving. 'I think we'd better get this show on the road Jock,' he said. They drank up and said their goodbyes to the funhouse of the Yorkshire Moors.

As they headed for the door, Annie called: 'Hold on a minute lads. Sign this before you go. You're honorary members of the Saturday Club.'

They collected Jock's car down the road and King said: 'Follow me over the tops. See you in the pub . . .'

He turned left down the M6 with a strange army of feelings fighting in his head. He was sad yet glad it was over. He wanted to get home to Maggie and the kids. But what now? The dole? Maybe Harris would give him a bit of freelance work.

It was five o'clock when the pair docked, in tandem, at the Majestic.

'I had a lump in my throat for miles,' admitted Jock as they took their familiar seat in the window. 'This is our last pint of one hell of a trip. What we going to do now pal?'

'Let the dust settle and we'll meet here on Monday lunch for a swift half. I've got to clean the camper up properly and take it back in the morning. Tonight, I'm going to leave it at home. Perhaps you'll give me a lift to the Dirty Duck to see if mine's still there. Or if it still goes.'

It was and it did. King thanked the gaffer and said he was taking it and would see him in a couple of days. Jock left his car in it's place and followed King to Orchard Avenue where the camper just squeezed into the drive. The garden was still neat and tidy. The kids raced out of the front door and gave him a royal welcome. Maggie followed more sedately and gave him a kiss. 'Welcome home love,' she said tearfully.

'Hey Jock, just help us in with some of this gear and I'll take you back for your car. Come in lad.'

All was flurry and excitement like a spring Christmas. 'Did you get us any rock dad?' Jock turned his eyes.

'I'll leave you folk. Just nip us down the Duck, Joe,' said Jock.

As he climbed out to go to his own car again the two lads shook hands. 'Was that the trip of a lifetime or what?' grinned King. 'Coming again?'

Jock's answer was lost in the ignition of his own company car. 'At least we've dodged the buggers so far,' he laughed, and drove home to his kinfolk.

King spent the evening in the warm glow of his own family and realised how much he had really missed it. He told them some of the stories. Maggie had bought rump steak and they opened a bottle of wine.

'Well, Pet, I hope you've got that out of your system,' she laughed . . .

He took Ross another bottle of Scotch when he returned the shining caravette that had been their home and HQ for so long. He regaled him with a few of the stories, joined him for a dram and waved goodbye.

Almost out of habit he rang Harris at eight thirty on Monday morning.

'You're not actually back are you?' asked the news editor. 'Well done chum. Had enough?'

'I think I have,' said King. 'Life's going to seem a bit flat from now on though.'

'Meet me at the Majestic at one fifteen and we'll have a spot of lunch. I've actually got a deputy who can stand in for an hour or so today.'

That suited King who was meeting Jock there anyway. He rang his mate and they made a date for midday.

'What are you up to now?' asked Maggie, nervously. 'Not off again?'

'No way,' said King. 'Just got to wrap it all with Harris over a bit of lunch. Then I reckon my journalising days are over.'

'Recovered, wee man?' grinned Jock cheekily. He obviously had.

'Just a bit liverish,' grinned King.

'I'm not surprised with your lifestyle.'

'Wouldn't have missed it for anything, Jock, God, some of those people up there. When you do a fast re-take it's almost unreal. There's some grand people around. Some crackpots. Some pathetic ones, but I was struck by the humour everyone seems to enjoy. You and me have been around pubs for years. But this sort of trip is a bit different from inspecting cooling systems, meeting targets and doling out beer mats.

'Maggie has kept all the cuttings. I'd almost forgotten some of the tales, you know. Don't get me wrong mate, it's great to be home, just great. But that little bit of freedom took me on a magic carpet.'

'I'll tell you what, we'll take the families up to meet our fellow members of the Saturday club in the summer.'

'Would that be wise?' smiled King. 'I'll give you a ring later, here's Keith Harris. The big winding up moment.' Jock left as Harris strolled over. They shook hands. 'Hey Joe, is that your mate Jock?'

'All of him,' laughed King.

Harris called: 'Jock!'

Jock went out of the revolving door and straight back in the other side. 'Yep?'

King said, 'Come and meet Keith Harris mate. He's responsible for all you've been through.'

'Perhaps you'll join us for a bit of lunch,' said the news editor. 'Enjoy the trip?'

'I was only the notebook carrier and a shoulder to laugh on,' shrugged Jock. 'But it was great. But for God's sake don't let him loose on the populace again. Maggie would murder you.'

Harris laughed as they sat at the dining table. 'That was great stuff Joe,' he said. 'The editor's delighted. Unfortunately there are no staff jobs at the moment. They're like gold-dust. All these graduates coming through, and they don't know whether to stand on the bucket or swing on the handle. They know the square root of sod all. They're not streetwise, you see. Heads full of learning and theory. They wouldn't know a good story if it strolled out and smacked them in the mouth.

But the Newspaper Proprietors' Association have some deal whereby they have to employ a high percentage of these dip sticks.

'But I'd be prepared to give you another roving commission if anything cropped up. Would you consider it?'

'Of course I would,' said King. 'But not yet for Christ's sake. And in the meantime I might get a proper day job.'

'I understand that,' said Harris. 'It's just that if I get any ideas, or you do, we could have a chat.'

Jock held his head in his hands and the other two laughed.

'It happens I do have a glimmering of an idea, but I'll work on it before I say anything.'

Jock excused himself and left the table to visit the gents.

'You serious Joe?' said Harris seriously.

'I might be. Let's let the dust settle while I mull it around. But it could be a good 'un.'

Harris laughed again and ordered three brandies. When Jock returned he saw the glasses and groaned: 'I'm going to have to knock this life style on the head.' When he had finished his brandy he stood, shook hands all round and said: 'I'll let you two have your chat in peace.'

'I think we've had it really Joe,' said Harris. He put his hand into his inside pocket and took out an envelope, handing it to King. 'The editor says thanks. So do I mate. The expenses must have been enormous. And there's a bit of a merit bonus too. I'll be seeing you.' And he was gone. King sat for a moment and put the envelope in his pocket without opening it.

Back at home peace reigned, as it usually did unless the kids got crotchety. But King could handle that – firmly.

Maggie met him, 'The end of the gallop Joe. Can you settle?'

'I have every confidence in fulfilling my duties to my family,' he said in mock seriousness.

'You daft so-and-so,' said Maggie giving him a hug. 'Thought about anything else yet?'

'Sexy!'

'I mean jobwise,' chided his wife. 'You know the old wolf and doorstop theory.'

'I'll start looking this week. There's no jobs on the Evening Press. Harris said he'd like to have fixed me up with something if he could. Something to do with undergraduates and buckets.'

Maggie looked at him strangely.

'Oh yes, I almost forgot. Keith gave me this when he left. I think it's cash. It's yours love.'

Maggie took the package somewhat nervously and slit it open with her sensible letter opener – a present from Margate with the town's coat of arms on the handle.

She put in her thumb and forefinger and carefully pulled out a wad of notes.

'God Joe, how much is there here?'

'Don't know Pet. Count it.'

Maggie did. 'It's four hundred quid Joe,' she gasped. 'What did Keith say it was for? You've drawn your expenses along the way.'

'He said it was a few quid more exes and a bonus payment by means of saying well done. Buy the kids and yourself something with it.'

'Things be damned. Let's have a super-duper weekend away, somewhere in the country.'

'Great,' sighed King. 'Just what I could do with.'